Fighting for the Right

Oliver Optic

Illustrated by A. B. Shute

ESPRIOS DIGITAL PUBLISHING

THE BLUE AND THE GRAY

By OLIVER OPTIC

FIGHTING FOR THE RIGHT

The Blue and the Gray Series

BY OLIVER OPTIC

FIGHTING FOR THE RIGHT

The Blue and the Gray Series

FIGHTING FOR THE RIGHT

by

OLIVER OPTIC

Author of "The Army and Navy Series" "Young America Abroad"
"The Great Western Series" "The Woodville Stories"
"The Starry Flag Series" "The Boat-Club Series"
"The Onward and Upward Series" "The Yacht-Club Series"
"The Lake Shore Series" "The Riverdale Stories"
"The Boat-Builder Series" "Taken by the Enemy"
"Within the Enemy's Lines" "On the Blockade"
"Stand by the Union" "A Missing Million"
"A Millionaire at Sixteen" etc., etc., etc.

To

My Grand Nephew

RICHARD LABAN ADAMS

This Book

Is Affectionately Dedicated

PREFACE

"FIGHTING FOR THE RIGHT" is the fifth and last but one of "The Blue and the Gray Series. " The character of the operations in connection with the war of the Rebellion, and the incidents in which the interest of the young reader will be concentrated, are somewhat different from most of those detailed in the preceding volumes of the series, though they all have the same patriotic tendency, and are carried out with the same devotion to the welfare of the nation as those which deal almost solely in deeds of arms.

Although the soldiers and sailors of the army and navy of the Union won all the honors gained in the field of battle or on the decks of the national ships, and deserved all the laurels they gathered by their skill and bravery in the trying days when the republic was in peril, they were not the only actors in the greatest strife of the nineteenth century. Not all the labor of "saving the Union" was done in the trenches, on the march, on the gun deck of a man-of-war, or in other military and naval operations, though without these the efforts of all others would have been in vain. Thousands of men and women who never "smelled gunpowder, " who never heard the booming cannon, or the rattling musketry, who never witnessed a battle on sea or land, but who kept their minds and hearts in touch with the holy cause, labored diligently and faithfully to support and sustain the soldiers and sailors at the front.

If all those who fought no battles are not honored like the leaders and commanders in the loyal cause, if they wear no laurels on their brows, if no monuments are erected to transmit their memory to posterity, if their names and deeds are not recorded in the Valhalla of the redeemed nation, they ought not to be disregarded and ignored. It was not on the field of strife alone in the South that the battle was fought and won. The army and the navy needed a moral, as well as a material support, which was cheerfully rendered by the great army of the people who never buckled on a sword, or shouldered a musket. Their work can not be summed up in deeds, for there was little or nothing that was brilliant and dazzling in their career. They need no monuments; but their work was necessary to the final and glorious result of the most terrible war of modern times.

No apology is necessary for placing the hero of the story and his skilful associate in a position at a distance from the actual field of battle. They were working for the salvation of the Union as effectively as they could have done in the din of the strife. They were "Fighting for the Right, " as they understood it, though it is not treason to say, thirty years later, that the people of the South were as sincere as those of the North; and they could hardly have fought and suffered to the extent they did if it had been otherwise.

The incidents of the volume are more various than in the preceding stories, which were so largely a repetition of battle scenes; but the hero is still as earnest as ever in the cause he loves. He attains a high position without any ambition to win it; for, like millions of others who gave the best years of their lives to sustain the Union, who suffered the most terrible hardships and privations, so many hundreds of thousands giving their lives to their country, Christy fought and labored for the cause, and not from any personal ambition. It is the young man's high character, his devotion to duty, rather than the incidents and adventures in which he is engaged, that render him worthy of respect, and deserving of the honors that were bestowed upon him. The younger participants in the war of the Rebellion, Christy Passford among the number, are beginning to be grizzled with the snows of fifty winters; but they are still rejoicing in "A Victorious Union. "

    William T. Adams.

    Dorchester, April 18, 1892.

"Christy seized him by the collar with both hands.

CONTENTS

CHAPTER I.
A Conference at Bonnydale

CHAPTER II.
A Complicated Case

CHAPTER III.
The Departure of the Chateaugay

CHAPTER IV.
Monsieur Gilfleur explains

CHAPTER V.
An Abundance of Evidence

CHAPTER VI.
The Boarding of the Ionian

CHAPTER VII.
A Bold Proposition

CHAPTER VIII.
A Notable Expedition

CHAPTER IX.
The Frenchman in Bermuda

CHAPTER X.
Important Information obtained

CHAPTER XI.
An Unexpected Rencontre

CHAPTER XII.
As Impracticable Scheme

CHAPTER XIII.
At the End of the Chase

CHAPTER XIV.
An Easy Victory

CHAPTER XV.
The Gentleman with a Grizzly Beard

CHAPTER XVI.
Among the Bahamas

CHAPTER XVII.
The Landing at New Providence

CHAPTER XVIII.
An Affray in Nassau

CHAPTER XIX.
An Old Acquaintance

CHAPTER XX.
A Band of Ruffians

CHAPTER XXI.
A Question of Neutrality

CHAPTER XXII.
On Board of the Snapper

CHAPTER XXIII.
The Chateaugay in the Distance

CHAPTER XXIV.
The Tables turned

CHAPTER XXV.
Captain Flanger in Irons

CHAPTER XXVI.
A Visit to Tampa Bay

CHAPTER XXVII.
Among the Keys of Tampa

CHAPTER XXVIII.
The Surrender of the Reindeer

CHAPTER XXIX.
Bringing out the Prize

CHAPTER XXX.
A Very Important Service

CHAPTER XXXI.
An Undesired Promotion

CHAPTER I

A CONFERENCE AT BONNYDALE

"Well, Christy, how do you feel this morning? " asked Captain Passford, one bright morning in April, at Bonnydale on the Hudson, the residence of the former owner of the Bellevite, which he had presented to the government.

"Quite well, father; I think I never felt any better in all my life, " replied Lieutenant Passford, of the United States Navy, recently commander of the little gunboat Bronx, on board of which he had been severely wounded in an action with a Confederate fort in Louisiana.

"Do you feel any soreness at the wound in your arm? " inquired the devoted parent with some anxiety.

"Not a particle, father. "

"Or at the one in your thigh? "

"Not the slightest bit of soreness. In fact, I have been ready to return to my duty at any time within the last month, " replied Christy very cheerfully. "It would be a shame for me to loiter around home any longer, when I am as able to plank the deck as I ever was. In truth, I think I am better and stronger than ever before, for I have had a long rest. "

"Your vacation has been none too long, for you were considerably run down, the doctor said, in addition to your two wounds, " added Captain Passford, senior; for the young man had held a command, and was entitled to the same honorary title as his father.

"These doctors sometimes make you think you are sicker than you really are, " said Christy with a laugh.

"But your doctor did not do so, for your mother and I both thought you were rather run out by your labors in the Gulf. "

"If I was, I am all right now. Do I look like a sick one? I weigh more than I ever did before in my life. "

Fighting for the Right

"Your mother has taken excellent care of you, and you certainly look larger and stronger than when you went to sea in the Bronx."

"But I am very tired of this inactive life. I have been assigned to the Bellevite as second lieutenant, a position I prefer to a command, for the reasons I have several times given you, father."

"I am certainly very glad to have you returned to the Bellevite, though the honors will be easier with you than they were when you were the commander of the Bronx."

"But I shall escape the responsibility of the command, and avoid being pointed at as one who commands by official influence," said Christy, rather warmly; for he felt that he had done his duty with the utmost fidelity, and it was not pleasant to have his hard-earned honors discounted by flings at his father's influence with the government.

"It is impossible to escape the sneers of the discontented, and there are always plenty of such in the navy and the army. But, Christy, you wrong yourself in taking any notice of such flings, for they have never been thrown directly at you, if at all. You are over-sensitive, and you have not correctly interpreted what your superiors have said to you," said Captain Passford seriously.

His father recalled some of the conversations between the young officer and Captain Blowitt and others, reported to him before. He insisted that the remarks of his superiors were highly complimentary to him, and that he had no right to take offence at them.

"I dare say I am entirely wrong, father; but it will do me no harm to serve in a subordinate capacity," added Christy.

"I agree with you here; but I must tell you again, as I have half a dozen times before, that I never asked a position or promotion for you at the Navy Department. You have won your honors and your advancement yourself," continued the father.

"Well, it was all the same, father; you have used your time and your money very freely in the service of the government, as you could not help doing. I know that I did my duty, and the department promoted me because I was your son," said Christy, laughing.

"Not at all, my son; you deserved your promotion every time, and if you had been the son of a wood-chopper in the State of Maine, you would have been promoted just the same, " argued Captain Passford.

"Perhaps I should, " answered the young officer rather doubtfully.

"After what you did in your last cruise with the Bronx, a larger and finer vessel would have been given to you in recognition of the brilliant service you had rendered, " added the father. "I prevented this from being done simply because you wished to take the position of second lieutenant on board of the Bellevite. "

"Then I thank you for it, father, " replied Christy heartily.

"But the department thinks it has lost an able commander, " continued the captain with a smile.

"I am willing to let the department think so, father. All I really ask of the officials now is to send me back to the Gulf, and to the Bellevite. I believe you said that I was to go as a passenger in the Chateaugay. "

"I did; and she has been ready for over a week. "

"Why don't she go, then? " asked Christy impatiently.

"On her way to the Gulf she is to engage in some special service, " replied Captain Passford, as he took some letters from his pocket.

"Letters! " exclaimed the young lieutenant, laughing as he recalled some such missives on two former occasions. "Do you still keep your three agents in the island of Great Britain? "

"I don't keep them, for they are now in the employ of the government, though they still report to me, and we use the system adopted some two years ago. "

"What is it this time, father? " asked Christy, his curiosity as well as his patriotism excited by this time at the prospect of capturing a Confederate man-of-war, or even a blockade-runner.

"There are traitors in and about the city of New York, " answered Captain Passford, as he returned the letters to his pocket. "We had a rebel in the house here at one time, you remember, and it is not quite prudent just now to explain the contents of the letters. "

"All right, father; but I suppose you will read them to me before I sail for the South. "

"I will talk to you about it another time, " added the captain, as a knock was heard at the door. "Come in! "

It was the man-servant of the house, and he brought in a tray on which there was a card, which Captain Passford took.

"Captain Wilford Chantor, " the captain read from the card. "Show him in, Gates. Lieutenant Chantor is appointed to the command of the Chateaugay, Christy, in which you take passage to the Gulf; but she will not go there directly. "

"Captain Chantor, " said Gates, as he opened the door for the visitor.

"I am happy to see you, Captain Chantor, though I have not had the pleasure of meeting you before, " said the captain, as he rose from his chair, and bowed to the gentleman, who was in the uniform of a lieutenant.

"I presume I have the honor to address Captain Horatio Passford, " said the visitor, as he took a letter from his pocket, bowing very respectfully at the same time, and delivering the letter.

"I am very glad to meet you, Captain Chantor, " continued Captain Passford, taking the hand of the visitor. "Allow me to introduce to you my son, Lieutenant Passford, who will be a passenger on your ship to the Gulf. "

"I am very happy to make your acquaintance, Mr. Passford, for I need hardly say that I have heard a great deal about you before, and this is a very unexpected pleasure, " replied Captain Chantor.

"Thank you, Captain, and I am equally happy to meet you, as I am to be a passenger on your ship, " added Christy, as they shook hands very cordially.

"I had three other passengers on board, but they have been transferred to the store-ship, which sails to-day, and you will be my only passenger."

"At my suggestion," said Captain Passford smiling, doubtless at the puzzled expression of the captain of the Chateaugay at his statement.

"I am to attend to some special service on my voyage to the Gulf, and I am ordered to take my instructions from you," added Captain Chantor.

"Precisely so; but I hold no official position, and your orders will be put in proper form before you sail," replied Christy's father. "Now, if you will be patient for a little while, I will explain the nature of the special service."

"I shall be very glad to understand the subject, and I am confident my patience will hold out to any extent you may require."

The conversation so far had taken place in the library. The owner of Bonnydale rose from his arm-chair, opened the door into the hall, and looked about him very cautiously. Then he closed a window which the unusual warmth of an April day had rendered it necessary to open. He conducted his companions to the part of the room farthest from the door, and seated them on a sofa, while he placed his arm-chair in front of them. Even Christy thought his father was taking extraordinary precautions, and the visitor could make nothing of it.

"As I have had occasion to remark before to-day, there are traitors in and about New York," the captain began.

"If you have any private business with Captain Chantor, father, I am perfectly willing to retire," suggested Christy.

"No; I wish you to understand this special service, for you may be called upon to take a hand in it," replied Captain Passford; and the son seated himself again. "There are traitors in and about New York, I repeat. I think we need not greatly wonder that some of the English people persist in attempting to run the blockade at the South, when some of our own citizens are indirectly concerned in the same occupation."

Fighting for the Right

This seemed to the captain of the Chateaugay an astounding statement, and not less so to Christy, and neither of them could make anything of it; but they were silent, concluding that the special service related to this matter.

"In what I am about to say to you, Captain Chantor, I understand that I am talking to an officer of the utmost discretion, " continued Captain Passford, "and not a word of it must be repeated to any person on board of the Chateaugay, and certainly not to any other person whatever. "

"I understand you perfectly, sir, " replied the officer. "My lips shall be sealed to all. "

"I wish to say that the command of the Chateaugay would have been offered to my son, but I objected for the reason that he prefers not to have a command at present, " said the captain.

"That makes it very fortunate for me. "

"Very true, though the change was not made for your sake. You were selected for this command as much on account of your discretion as for your skill and bravery as an officer. "

"I consider myself very highly complimented by the selection. "

"Now to the point: I have information that a fast steamer, intended to carry eight guns, called the Ovidio, sailed from the other side of the ocean some time since, and she is to be a vessel in the Confederate navy. Her first port will be Nassau, New Providence. "

"Does that prove that any Americans are traitors in and about New York, father? " asked Christy.

"She is to run the blockade with a cargo consisting in part of American goods. "

Captain Passford took a file of papers from his pocket.

CHAPTER II

A COMPLICATED CASE

Captain Passford looked over his papers for a moment; but it was soon evident from his manner that he had secrets which he would not intrust even to his son, unless it was necessary to do so. He seemed to be armed with documentary evidence upon which to act, but he did not read any of his papers, and soon returned them to his pocket.

"The American goods of which I speak are certain pieces of machinery to be used in the manufacture of arms, " continued the captain. "They cannot be obtained in England, and the traitors have decided to send them direct, rather than across the ocean in the first instance. These will form the principal and most important part of the cargo of a steamer now loaded, though she will carry other goods, such as the enemy need most at the present time. "

"I did not suppose any Americans were wicked enough to engage in such an enterprise for the sake of making money, " said Christy indignantly.

"The steamer of which you speak is already loaded, is she? " asked Captain Chantor.

"She is; and now I wish both of you to go with me, and I will point out the vessel to you, and you must mark her so well that you can identify her when occasion requires. "

The trio left the house and took the train together. They went to New York, and in an out-of-the-way locality they went down to a wharf; but there was no steamer or vessel of any kind there, and the pier was falling to pieces from decay. Captain Passford stopped short, and seemed to be confounded when he found the dock was not occupied.

"I am afraid we are too late, and that the steamer has sailed on her mission of destruction, " said he, almost overcome by the discovery. "She was here last night, and was watched till this morning. She has already cleared, bound to Wilmington, Delaware, with a cargo of old iron. "

"Do you know her name, Captain Passford? " asked the commander of the Chateaugay.

"She was a screw steamer of about six hundred tons, and was called the Ionian, but she is American. "

It was useless to remain there any longer, for the steamer certainly was not there. Captain Passford hailed a passing-tug-boat, and they were taken on board. The master of the boat was instructed to steam down the East River, and the party examined every steamer at anchor or under way. The tug had nearly reached the Battery before the leader of the trio saw any vessel that looked like the Ionian. The tug went around this craft, for she resembled the one which had been in the dock, and the name indicated was found on her stern.

"I breathe easier, for I was afraid she had given us the slip, " said Captain Passford. "She is evidently all ready to sail. "

"The Chateaugay is in commission, and ready to sail at a moment's notice, " added her commander.

"But you are not ready to leave at once, Christy, " suggested Captain Passford, with some anxiety in his expression.

"Yes, I am, father; I put my valises on board yesterday, and when mother and Florry went down to Mr. Pembroke's I bade them both good-by, for after I have waited so long for my passage, I felt that the call would come in a hurry, " replied Christy. "I am all ready to go on board of the Chateaugay at this moment. "

"And so am I, " added Captain Chantor.

"But I am not ready with your orders in full, though they are duly signed, " said Captain Passford. "I will put you on shore at the foot of Atlantic Avenue in Brooklyn, Captain Chantor, and you will hasten to your ship, get up steam, and move down to this vicinity. I will put my son on board as soon as I can have your papers completed. "

The order necessary to carry out this procedure was given to the captain of the tug, and the commander of the Chateaugay was landed at the place indicated. The tug started for the other side of the river.

"It seems to me this is very strange business, father," said Christy, as he and his father seated themselves at the stern of the boat.

"Traitors do not work in the daylight, my son, as you have learned before this time," replied Captain Passford.

"If you know the men who are engaged in supplying the enemy with machinery, why do you not have them arrested and put in Fort Lafayette?" asked Christy, in a very low tone, after he had assured himself that no person was within possible hearing distance. "It looks as though the case might be settled here, without going to sea to do it."

"We have not sufficient evidence to convict them; and to make arrests without the means of conviction would be worse than doing nothing. The Ionian has cleared for Wilmington with a cargo of old iron. Everything looks regular in regard to her, and I have no doubt there is some party who would claim the castings if occasion required. The first thing to be ascertained is whether or not the steamer goes to Wilmington."

"Then we can make short work of her."

"My information in regard to this treason comes from Warnock — you know who he is?"

"Captain Barnes," replied Christy promptly, for the names of all the agents of his father in England and Scotland had been given to him on a former occasion, when the information received from one of the three had resulted in the capture of the Scotian and the Arran.

"Barnes is a very shrewd man. He does not inform me yet in what manner he obtained the information that the Ovidio was to carry this machinery from Nassau into a rebel port; but I shall get it later in a letter. He gave me the name of the party who was to furnish the machinery; and one of his agents obtained this from the direction of a letter to New York. I placed four skilful detectives around this man, who stands well in the community. They have worked the case admirably, and spotted the Ionian. I have aided them in all possible ways; but the evidence is not complete. If this steamer proceeds beyond Wilmington, Captain Chantor will be instructed to capture her and send her back to New York."

"Then this business will soon be settled, " added Christy.

"Perhaps not; the government official, with authority to act, is in New York. I shall see him at once. I have no doubt the detectives have already reported that the Ionian has moved down the river, " said Captain Passford, as the tug came up to a pier, where father and son landed.

They went to an office in Battery Place, where the captain was informed that a special messenger had been sent to Bonnydale to acquaint him with the fact that the Ionian had moved down the river. Files of documents, containing reports of detectives and other papers, were examined and compared, and then the government official proceeded to finish the filling out of Captain Chantor's orders. The paper was given to Christy, with an order to deliver it to the commander of the Chateaugay. The tug had been detained for them, and they hastened on board of her.

They found the suspected steamer at her moorings still; but it was evident that she was preparing to weigh her anchor. The tug continued on her course towards the Navy Yard, and the Chateaugay was discovered in the berth she had occupied for the last two weeks. Everything looked lively on board of her, as though she were getting ready to heave up her anchor.

"Christy, you will find on board of your steamer a man by the name of Gilfleur, " said Captain Passford, as the tug approached the man-of-war.

"That sounds like a French name, " interposed Christy.

"It is a French name, and the owner of it is a Frenchman who has been a detective in Paris. He has accomplished more in this matter than all the others put together, and he will go with you, for you will find in the commander's instructions that you have more than one thing to do on your way to the Gulf. I gave him a letter to you. "

"I shall be glad to see him. "

"Now, my son, we must part, for I have business on shore, and you may have to sail at any moment, " said Captain Passford, as he took the two hands of his son. "I have no advice to give you except to be prudent, and on this duty to be especially discreet. That's all—good-by."

They parted, after wringing each other's hands, as they had parted several times before. They might never meet again in this world, but both of them subdued their emotion, for they were obeying the high and solemn call of duty; both of them were fighting for the right, and the civilian as well as the naval officer felt that it was his duty to lay down his life for his suffering country. Christy mounted the gangway, and was received by Captain Chantor on the quarter-deck. He had been on board before, and had taken possession of his stateroom.

The passenger took from his pocket the files of papers given him by the official on shore; and then he noticed for the first time an envelope addressed to him. The commander retired to his cabin to read his instructions, and Christy went to his stateroom in the ward room to open the envelope directed to him. As soon as he broke the seal he realized that his father had done a great deal of writing, and he had no doubt the paper contained full instructions for him, as well as a history of the difficult case in which he was to take a part. A paper signed by the official informed him that he was expected to occupy a sort of advisory position near the commander of the Chateaugay, though of course he was in no manner to control him in regard to the management of the ship.

Christy read his father's letter through. The government was exceedingly anxious to obtain accurate information in regard to the state of affairs at Nassau, that hot-bed for blockade-runners. The Chateaugay was to look out for the Ovidio, whose ultimate destination was Mobile, where she was to convey the gun-making machinery, and such other merchandise as the traitorous merchant of New York wished to send into the Confederacy. The name of this man was given to him, and it was believed that papers signed by him would be found on board of the Ionian.

A knock at the door of his room disturbed his examination of the documents, and he found the commander of the steamer there. After looking about the ward room, and into the adjoining staterooms, he came in without ceremony.

"Here is my hand, Mr. Passford," said he, suiting the action to the word. "I find after reading my instructions that I am expected to consult with you, and as I have the very highest respect and regard for you after the brilliant record you have made" —

"Don't you believe that I won my promotion to my present rank through the influence of my father? " demanded Christy, laughing pleasantly, as he took the offered hand and warmly pressed it.

"If you did, your father did the very best thing in the world for his country, and has given it one of the bravest and best officers in the service, " replied Captain Chantor, still wringing the hand of his passenger. "But I don't believe anything of the kind; and no officer who knows you, even if he is thirsting for promotion, believes it. I have heard a great many of higher rank than either of us speak of you, and if you had been present your ears would have tingled; but I never heard a single officer of any rank suggest that you owed your rapid advancement to anything but your professional skill and your unflinching bravery, as well as to your absolute and hearty devotion to your country. I rank you in date, Mr. Passford, but I would give a great deal to have your record written against my name. "

"Your praise is exceedingly profuse, Captain Chantor, but I must believe you are honest, however unworthy I may be of your unstinted laudation, " said Christy with his eyes fixed on the floor, and blushing like a school-girl.

"I hope and believe there will be no discount on our fellowship. A man came on board this afternoon, and gives me a letter from the proper authority, referring me to you in regard to his mission. "

Christy decided to see this person at once.

CHAPTER III

THE DEPARTURE OF THE CHATEAUGAY

The commander told Christy that he would probably find the person who had brought the letter to him in the waist, for he knew nothing of his quality, position, or anything else about him, and he did not know where to berth him, though there was room enough in the ward room or the steerage. He was dressed like a gentleman, and brought two very handsome valises on board with him.

"For all that, I did not know but that he might be a French cook, a steward, or something of that sort, " added Captain Chantor, laughing.

"He is a man who is said to be a Napoleon in his profession; but I will tell you all about him after we get under way, for I am in a hurry to speak with him, " replied Christy.

"He is evidently a Frenchman, " continued the captain.

"He is; but I never saw him in my life, and know nothing about him except what I have learned from a long letter my father gave me when I was coming on board. "

"I have been told that you speak French like a native of Paris, Mr. Passford, " suggested the commander.

"Not so bad as that; I have studied the language a great deal under competent instructors from Paris, but I am not so proficient as you may think, though I can make my way with those who speak it, " replied the passenger, as he moved towards the door of the stateroom.

"And I can't speak the first word of it, for I have been a sailor all my life, though I went through the naval academy somewhat hurriedly," continued the commander.

"Fortunately you don't need French on the quarter-deck; " and Christy left the stateroom.

Fighting for the Right

The captain went into his cabin, but came out before the passenger could reach the deck. He informed Christy that he was directed to heave short on the anchor and watch for a signal mentioned, which was to be hoisted near the Battery. He might get under way at any minute.

Christy found the person of whom the captain had spoken in the waist. He was dressed in a black suit, and looked more like a dandy than a detective. He was apparently about forty years of age, rather slenderly built, but with a graceful form. He wore a long black mustache, but no other beard. He was pacing the deck, and seemed to be very uneasy, possibly because he was all alone, for no one took any notice of him, though the captain had received him very politely.

"Monsieur Gilfleur? " said Christy, walking up to him, and bowing as politely as a Parisian.

"I am Mr. Gilfleur; have I the honor to address Lieutenant Passford?" replied the Frenchman.

"I am Lieutenant Passford, though I have no official position on board of this steamer. "

"I am aware of it, " added Mr. Gilfleur, as he chose to call himself, taking a letter from the breast pocket of his coat, and handing it very gracefully to Christy.

"Pardon me, " added the young officer, as he opened the missive.

It was simply a letter of introduction from Captain Passford, intended to assure him of the identity of the French detective. Mr. Gilfleur evidently prided himself on his knowledge of the English language, for he certainly spoke it fluently and correctly, though with a little of the accent of his native tongue.

"I am very happy to meet you, Mr. Gilfleur, " said Christy in French, as he extended his hand to the other, who promptly took it, and from that moment seemed to lose all his embarrassment.

"I thank you, Mr. Passford, for this pleasant reception, for it is possible that we may have a great deal of business together, and I hope you have confidence in me. "

Fighting for the Right

"Unlimited confidence, sir, since my father heartily indorses you."

"I thank you, sir, and I am sure we shall be good friends, though I am not a gentleman like you, Mr. Passford."

"You are my equal in every respect, for though my father is a very rich man, I am not. But we are all equals in this country."

"I don't know about that," said the Frenchman, with a Parisian shrug of the shoulders. "Your father has treated me very kindly, and I have heard a great deal about his brave and accomplished son," said Mr. Gilfleur, with a very deferential bow.

"Spare me!" pleaded Christy, with a deprecatory smile and a shake of the head.

"You are very modest, Mr. Passford, and I will not offend you. I am not to speak of our mission before the Chateaugay is out of sight of land," said the detective, looking into the eyes of the young man with a gaze which seemed to reach the soul, for he was doubtless measuring the quality and calibre of his associate in the mission, as he called it, in which both were engaged. "I knew your father very well in Paris," he added, withdrawing his piercing gaze.

"Then you are the gentleman who found the stewardess of the Bellevite when she ran away with a bag of French gold at Havre?" said Christy, opening his eyes.

"I have the honor to be that person," replied Mr. Gilfleur, with one of his graceful bows. "It was a difficult case, for the woman was associated with one of the worst thieves of Paris, and it took me a month to run them down."

"Though I was a small boy, I remember it very well, for I was on board of the Bellevite at the time," replied Christy. "I know that he was very enthusiastic in his praise of the wonderful skill of the person who recovered the money and sent the two thieves to prison. I understand now why my father sent to Paris for you when he needed a very skilful person of your profession."

"Thank you, Mr. Passford; you know me now, and we shall be good friends."

"No doubt of it; but here comes the captain, and I have a word to say to him, " added Christy, as he touched his naval cap to the commander. "Allow me to introduce to you my friend Mr. Gilfleur, whom my father employed in Havre six years ago. "

The captain was as polite as the Frenchman, and gave him a hearty reception. Christy then suggested that his friend should be berthed in the ward room. The ship's steward was called, and directed to give Mr. Gilfleur a room next to the other passenger. As they were likely to have many conferences together in regard to the business on their hands, they were both particular in regard to the location of their rooms; and the chief steward suited them as well as he could.

The detective spoke to him in French, but the steward could not understand a word he said. Christy inquired if any of the ward-room officers spoke the polite language, for his friend might sometimes wish to converse in his own tongue.

"I don't believe they do, for they all got into the ward room through the hawse-hole, " replied the steward, laughing at the very idea.

When the passengers went on deck, the commander introduced them both to the officers of the ship. To each in turn, at the request of Christy, he put the question as to whether or not he could speak French; and they all replied promptly in the negative, and laughed at the inquiry.

"Have you no one on board who speaks French, Captain Chantor? " asked Christy.

"I don't know anything about it, but as it seems to be of some importance to you and your friend, I will ascertain at once. Mr. Suppleton, will you overhaul the ship's company, and see if you can find any one that speaks French, " continued the commander, addressing the chief steward.

In about half an hour he returned, and reported that he was unable to find a single person who could speak a word of French. Doubtless many of the officers, who were of higher grade than any on board of the Chateaugay, were fluent enough in the language, but they were not to be found in the smaller vessels of the navy; for, whatever their rank before the war, they had all been advanced to the higher positions. Every one of the officers on board of this steamer had been the captain of a vessel, and had been instructed in the profession after the war began. Though substantially educated, they were not to be compared in this respect with the original officers.

"We can talk as much as we please of our mission after we get out of sight of land; and as long as we do it in French, no one will understand us, " said Christy to his fellow-passenger.

"As soon as we are permitted by my orders to do so, I shall have much to say to you, Mr. Passford, " replied Mr. Gilfleur.

"On deck! " shouted a man in the mizzen-top.

"Aloft! " returned Mr. Birdwing, the first lieutenant.

"Signal over the boarding-station, sir! " reported the quartermaster in the top. "It is a number—'Get under way!'"

The executive officer reported the signal to the commander, though he was on deck, and had heard the words of the quartermaster.

"Get under way at once, Mr. Birdwing, " said the captain.

"Boatswain, all hands up anchor! " said the first lieutenant to this officer; and in a moment the call rang through the ship.

Every officer and seaman was promptly in his station, for it was a welcome call. The ship's company were dreaming of prize-money, for officers had made fabulous sums from this source. In one instance a lieutenant received for his share nearly forty thousand dollars; and even an ordinary seaman pocketed seventeen hundred from a single capture. The Chateaugayans were anxious to engage in this harvest, and in a hurry to be on their way to the field of fortune.

In a short time the steamer was standing down East River at moderate speed. The Ionian could not be seen yet, and nothing in regard to her was known to any one on board except the captain and his two passengers. As the ship approached the battery, a tug, which Christy recognized as the one his father had employed, came off and hailed the Chateaugay. The screw was stopped, and Captain Passford was discovered at her bow. He waved his hat to his son, saluted the commander in the same manner, and then passed up an envelope.

The tug sheered off, and the ship continued on her course, with a pilot at the wheel. The missive from the shore was addressed to Captain Chantor. He opened it at once, and then ordered one bell to be rung to stop her. A few moments later a heavy tug came off, and twelve men were put on board, with an order signed by the government official for the commander to receive them on board. There had evidently been some afterthoughts on shore. These men were turned in with the crew, except two who were officers, and they were put in the ward room. The ship then proceeded on her course.

"The Ionian is about two miles ahead of us, Mr. Passford," said the captain, after he had used his glass diligently for some time. And he spoke in a very low tone.

"We have no business with her at present," added Christy.

"None, except to watch her; and, fortunately, we have fine, clear weather, so that will not be a difficult job. By the way, Mr. Passford, the envelope I received was from your father, and he gives me information of another steamer expected in the vicinity of Bermuda about this time; and he thinks we had better look for her when she comes out from those islands," said the captain, evidently delighted with the prospect before him.

"What are these men for that were sent off in the tug?" Christy inquired; for he felt that he had a right to ask the question.

"They are to take the Ionian back to New York, if we have to capture her."

Captain Passford appeared to be afraid the Chateaugay would be shorthanded if she had to send a prize crew home with the Ionian.

CHAPTER IV

MONSIEUR GILFLEUR EXPLAINS

The two officers and ten men that had been sent off to the Chateaugay after she got under way, had evidently been considered necessary by the authorities on shore after the receipt of the intelligence that another vessel for the Confederates had been sent to Bermuda. A steamer had arrived that day from Liverpool, and Captain Passford must have received his mail after he landed from the tug. Captain Chantor had waited several hours for the signal to get under way, and there had been time enough to obtain the reinforcement from the Navy Yard.

The officer in command of the detachment of sailors said that he had been ordered to follow the Chateaugay, and he had been provided with a fast boat for this purpose. The steamer proceeded on her course as soon as the transport boat had cast off her fasts, and everything suddenly quieted down on board of her. The distance between the Ionian and the man-of-war was soon reduced to about a mile. It was beginning to grow dark, but the crew had been stationed and billed while the ship lay off the Navy Yard; but the new hands sent on board were assigned to watches and quarter-watches, stationed and billed, as though they were a part of the regular ship's company. One of the two additional officers was placed in each of the watches.

Before it was really dark everything on board was in order, and the ship was put in perfect trim. Christy could not help seeing that Captain Chantor was a thorough commander, and that his officers were excellent in all respects. He walked about the ship, wishing to make himself familiar with her. His father had not written to him in regard to the second vessel which the Chateaugay was to look out for in the vicinity of the Bermuda Islands, and he only knew what the captain had told him in regard to the matter.

If the steamer was armed, as probably she was, an action would be likely to come off, and the young lieutenant could not remain idle while a battle was in prospect. His quick eye enabled him to take in all he saw without much study, and only one thing bothered him. In the waist, secured on blocks, was something like the ordinary whaleboat used in the navy; but it was somewhat larger than those

Fighting for the Right

with which he was familiar in the discharge of his duties, and differed in other respects from them. The first watch would begin at eight o'clock, and all hands were still on duty.

"What do you call this boat, Mr. Carlin? " asked Christy, as the third lieutenant was passing him.

"I call it a nondescript craft, " replied the officer, laughing. "It is something like a whaleboat, but it isn't one. "

"What is it for? " inquired the passenger.

"That is more than I know, sir. It was put on deck while we were still at the Navy Yard. I never saw a boat just like it before, and I have not the remotest idea of its intended use. Probably the captain can inform you. "

Christy was no wiser than before, but his curiosity was excited. He strolled to the quarter-deck, where he found the captain directing his night-glass towards the Ionian, which showed her port light on the starboard hand, indicating that the Chateaugay was running ahead of her. The commander called the second lieutenant, and gave him the order for the chief engineer to reduce the speed of the ship.

"The Ionian is a slow boat; at least, she is not as fast as the Chateaugay, Mr. Passford, " said Captain Chantor, when Christy had halted near him.

"That is apparent, " replied Christy. "How many knots can you make in your ship, Captain Chantor? "

"I am told that she has made fifteen when driven at her best. "

"That is more than the average of the steamers in the service by three knots, " added Christy. "I have just been forward, Captain, and I saw there a boat which is not quite on the regulation pattern. "

"It is like a whaleboat, though it differs from one in some respects, " added the commander.

"Is it for ordinary service, Captain Chantor? "

Fighting for the Right

"There you have caught me, for I don't know to what use she is to be applied, " replied the captain, laughing because, as the highest authority on board of the ship, he was unable to answer the question.

"You don't know? " queried Christy. "Or have I asked an indiscreet question? " said the passenger.

"If I knew, and found it necessary to conceal my knowledge from you, I should say so squarely, Mr. Passford, " added the commander, a little piqued. "I would not resort to a lie. "

"I beg your pardon, Captain Chanter; I certainly meant no offence, " pleaded Christy.

"No offence, Mr. Passford; my hand upon it, " said the commander, and they exchanged a friendly grip of the hands. "I really know nothing at all in regard to the intended use of the boat; in my orders, I am simply directed to place it at the disposal of Mr. Gilfleur at such time and place as he may require, and to co-operate with him in any enterprise in which he may engage. I must refer you to the French gentleman for any further information. "

The passenger went below to the ward room. The door of the detective's room was closed, and he knocked. He was admitted, and there he found Mr. Gilfleur occupied with a file of papers, which he was busily engaged in studying. In the little apartment were two middle-sized valises, which made it look as though the detective expected to pass some time on his present voyage to the South.

"I hope I don't disturb you, Mr. Gilfleur, " said Christy in French.

"Not at all, Mr. Passford; I am glad to see you, for I am ordered to consult very freely with you, and to inform you fully in regard to all my plans, " replied the Frenchman.

"Perhaps you can tell me, then, what that boat in the waist is for, " Christy began, in a very pleasant tone, and in his most agreeable manner, perhaps copying to some extent the Parisian suavity, as he had observed it in several visits he had made to the gay capital.

"I can tell you all about it, Mr. Passford, though that is my grand secret. No other person on board of this ship knows what it is for;

but you are my confidant, though I never had one before in the practice of my profession, " replied Mr. Gilfleur, fixing his keen gaze upon his associate. "A man's secret is the safest when he keeps it to himself. But I will tell you all about it. "

"No! no! I don't wish you to do that, Mr. Gilfleur, if you deem it wise to keep the matter to yourself, " interposed Christy. "My curiosity is a little excited, but I can control it. "

"I shall tell you all about it, for this affair is different from the ordinary practice of my profession, " replied the detective; and he proceeded to give a history of the boat in the waist, and then detailed the use to which it was to be applied.

"I am quite satisfied, and I should be glad to take part in the expedition in which you intend to use it, " said Christy when the explanation in regard to the boat was finished.

"You would be willing to take part in my little enterprise! " exclaimed the Frenchman, his eyes lighting up with pleasure.

"I should; why not? "

"Because it may be very dangerous, and a slight slip may cost us both our lives, " replied the detective very impressively, and with another of his keen and penetrating glances.

"I have not been in the habit of keeping under cover in my two years' service in the navy, and I know what danger is, " added Christy.

"I know you are a very brave young officer, Mr. Passford, but this service is very different from that on the deck of a ship of war in action. But we will talk of that at a future time, " said Mr. Gilfleur, as he rose hastily from his arm-chair at the desk, and rushed out into the ward room.

Christy had heard footsteps outside of the door, and he followed his companion. They found there Mr. Suppleton, the ship's steward, with the two extra officers who had been sent on board.

"Do you speak French, gentlemen? " asked the detective, addressing himself to the two officers.

Fighting for the Right

"Not a word of it," replied Mr. Gwyndale, one of them.

"Not a syllable of it," added Mr. Tempers, the other.

"Excuse me, gentlemen," said Mr. Gilfleur, as he retreated to his room.

Mr. Suppleton introduced the two new officers to Christy, and he then followed his associate. The Frenchman was afraid the newcomers understood his native language, and had been listening to his explanation of the use of the strange boat; but he had spoken in a whisper, and no one could have heard him, even if the listener had been a Frenchman.

"We are all right," said the detective when they had both resumed their seats, and the Frenchman had begun to overhaul his papers.

Mr. Gilfleur proceeded to explain in what manner he had obtained his knowledge of the plot to send the gun-making machinery to the South. One of Captain Passford's agents had ascertained the name of Hillman Davis, who was in correspondence with those who were fitting out the ships for the Confederate service.

"But that is all we learned from the letters—that the men who were sending out the ships were in correspondence with this man Davis, who is a very respectable merchant of New York," Mr. Gilfleur proceeded.

"Is that all you had to start with, my friend?" asked Christy.

"That was all; and it was very little. Your American detectives are more cautious than Frenchmen in the same service."

"I don't see how in the world you could work up the case with nothing more than a mere name to begin with," added Christy, beginning to have a higher opinion than ever of the skill of the French detective.

"I tell you it was a narrow foundation on which to work up the case. It may amuse you, but I will tell you how it was done. In the first place, Captain Passford gave me all the money I needed to work with. I applied for a situation at Mr. Davis's warehouse. He imported wines and liquors from France; when his corresponding clerk, who spoke and wrote French, was commissioned as a lieutenant in the army, he was looking for a man to take his place. He employed me. I had charge of the letters, and carried the mail to him in his private counting-room every time it came. "

"I don't believe that any of our American detectives would have been competent to take such a position, " suggested Christy, deeply interested in the narrative.

"That is where I had the advantage of them. I was well educated, and was graduated from the University of France, with the parchment in that valise, signed by the minister of education. The carrier brought all the letters to my desk. I looked them over, and when I found any from England or Scotland, or even France, I opened and read them. "

"How could you do that? " asked Christy curiously.

"I was educated to be a lawyer; but before I entered upon the profession, I found I had a taste for the detective service. I did some amateur work first, and was very successful. I afterwards reached a high position in the service of the government. I acquired a great deal of skill in disguising myself, and in all the arts of the profession. I could open and reseal a letter so that no change could be discovered in its appearance, and this was what I did in the service of Mr. Davis. He was a mean man, the stingiest I ever met, and he was as dishonest and unscrupulous as a Paris thief. I copied all the letters connected with the case I had in hand, and this enabled me to get to the bottom of the traitor's plot. He wrote letters himself, not only to England and Scotland, but to people in the South, sending them to Bermuda and Nassau. I took copies of all these, and saved one or two originals. My pay was so small that I resigned my situation, " and he flourished a great file of letters as he finished.

CHAPTER V

AN ABUNDANCE OF EVIDENCE

Captain Passford had certainly kept his own counsel with punctilious care; for he had never even mentioned the skilful detective in his family, though the members of it had met the gentleman in Paris and in Havre. Mr. Gilfleur was in constant communication with him while he was working up the exposure of the treason of Davis, who might have been a relative of the distinguished gentleman at the head of the Southern Confederacy, though there was no evidence to this effect.

"If the captain of this steamer manages his affair well with the Ionian, I expect to find letters on board of her signed by Davis, " continued Mr. Gilfleur. "From the information I obtained, your father put American detectives on the scent of Davis, who dogged him day and night till they found the Ionian, and ascertained in what manner she obtained her cargo; but she had been partly loaded before they reached a conclusion, and it is suspected that she has arms under the pieces of machinery, perhaps cannon and ammunition. "

The detective continued to explain his operations at greater length than it is necessary to report them. Christy listened till nearly midnight, and then he went on deck to ascertain the position of the chase before he turned in. He found the captain on the quarter-deck, vigilant and faithful to his duty, and evidently determined that the Ionian should not elude him.

"You are up late, Mr. Passford, " said the captain, when he recognized his passenger in the gloom of the night.

"I have been busy, and I came on deck to see where the Ionian was before I turned in, " replied Christy.

"I think the rascal has a suspicion that we have some business with him, for at four bells he turned his head in for the shore, " added the commander. "If you go forward you will see that we have dowsed every glim on board, even to our mast-head and side lights. "

"You are carrying no starboard and port light? "

"None; but we have a strong lookout aloft, and in every other available place. When the chase headed for the shore, we kept on our course for half an hour, and then put out the lights. We came about and went off to the eastward for another half-hour. Coming about, we went to the westward till we made her out, for she has not extinguished her lights. It is dark enough to conceal the ship from her, and no doubt she thinks we are still far to the southward of her. At any rate, she has resumed her former course, which was about south, half west."

Christy was satisfied with this explanation, for the Ionian was doing just what she was expected to do. She was not inclined to be overhauled by a gunboat, and she had attempted to dodge the Chateaugay: Besides, if she were bound to Wilmington, as her clearance stated, she would turn to the south-west two or three points by this time. The young officer seated himself in his room, and figured on the situation. If the steamer were making an honest voyage she would not be more than twenty miles off Absecum light at this time, and ought to be within ten of the coast.

At two bells Christy was still in his chair, and when he heard the bells he decided to go on deck again, for he felt that the time would soon come to settle every doubt in regard to the character of the Ionian. He found the commander still at his post, and he looked out for the chase. It was not more than a mile distant, and hardly to be seen in the gloom of a dark night.

"On deck again, Mr. Passford?" said Captain Chantor.

"Yes, sir; I am too much interested in this affair to sleep; besides, I feel as though I had slept at home enough to last me six months," replied the passenger. "It seems to me that the question of that vessel's destination is to be decided about this time, or at least within an hour or two."

Christy explained the calculation he had been making, in which the captain agreed with him, and declared that he had been over the same course of reasoning. Both of them thought the Ionian would not wait till daylight to change her course, as it would be more perilous to do so then than in the darkness.

"I am confident that she has not seen the Chateaugay since we put out the lights," said the captain. "At the present moment we must be off Absecum; but we cannot see the light. She is far off her course for Wilmington."

"That is plain enough."

"What she will do depends upon whether or not she suspects that a man-of-war is near her. We shall soon know, for she is already in a position to justify her capture."

"Better make sure of her course before that is done," suggested Christy, who felt that he was permitted to say as much as this.

"I don't intend to act till we are south of Cape Henlopen," added the commander promptly. "Before we do anything, I shall formally consult you, Mr. Passford, as I am advised to do."

"I shall be happy to serve as a volunteer, and I will obey your orders without question, and as strictly as any officer on board."

"That is handsome, considering the position in which you have been placed on board, Mr. Passford, and I appreciate the delicacy of your conduct."

Christy remained on deck another hour, and at the end of that time a quartermaster came aft to report that the chase had changed her course farther to the eastward. This proved to be the fact on examination by the officers on the quarter-deck, and as nearly as could be made out she was now headed to the south-east.

"But that will not take her to the Bahama Islands," suggested Christy.

"Certainly not; and she may not be bound to Nassau, as stated in those letters. But it is useless to speculate on her destination, for we shall be in condition in the morning to form an opinion," replied the captain. "I shall keep well astern of her till morning; and if there should be any change in her movements, I will have you called, Mr. Passford."

Christy considered this a sage conclusion, and he turned in on the strength of it. He was not disturbed during the remaining hours of the night. He had taken more exercise than usual that day, and he slept soundly, as he was in the habit of doing. The bell forward indicated eight o'clock when he turned out. Breakfast was all ready, but he hastened on deck to ascertain the position of the chase. The captain was not on the quarter-deck, but the first lieutenant was planking the deck for his morning "constitutional."

"Good-morning, Mr. Birdwing," said Christy.

"Good-morning, Mr. Passford; I hope you are very well this morning," replied the executive officer.

"Quite well, I thank you, sir. But what has become of the chase?" asked the passenger, for the Ionian did not appear to be in sight, and he began to be anxious about her.

"Still ahead of us, sir; but she cannot be seen without a glass. I was called with the morning watch, when the captain turned in. His policy is to keep the Ionian so that we may know just where she is, and also to give her the idea that she is running away from us," replied Mr. Birdwing, as he took a glass from the brackets and handed it to Christy.

The young officer could just make out the steamer with the aid of the glass. The Chateaugay was following her; and a glance at the compass gave her course as south-east, half south. Christy had sailed the Bronx over this course, and he knew where it would bring up.

"It is plain enough, Mr. Birdwing, that the Ionian is not bound to Nassau," said he.

"So Captain Chantor said when I came on deck," replied the first lieutenant.

"And it is equally plain where she is bound," added Christy. "That course means the Bermuda Islands, and doubtless that is her destination."

"So the captain said."

The passenger was satisfied, and went below for his breakfast. He found Mr. Gilfleur at the table; and as the fact that the Chateaugay was chasing the Ionian was well understood in the ward room, Christy did not hesitate to tell him the news. The Frenchman bestowed one of his penetrating glances upon his associate, and said nothing. After the meal was finished they retired to the detective's room. Mr. Gilfleur looked over his papers very industriously for a few minutes.

"This affair is not working exactly as it should, " said he, as he selected a letter from his files. "I supposed this steamer would proceed directly to Nassau. Read this letter, Mr. Passford. "

"Colonel Richard Pierson! " exclaimed Christy, as he saw to whom the letter was addressed.

"Anything strange about the address? " asked the detective.

"Perhaps nothing strange; but I saw this gentleman in Nassau two years ago, " replied Christy, as he recalled the events of his first trip to Mobile in the Bellevite. "I can say of my own knowledge that he is a Confederate agent, and was trying to purchase vessels there. This letter is signed by Hillman Davis. "

"The American traitor, " added Mr. Gilfleur; and both of them were using the French language.

"He says he shall send the machinery and other merchandise to Nassau to be reshipped to Mobile, " continued Christy, reading the letter. "He adds that he has bought the steamer Ionian for this purpose, and he expects to be paid in full for her. I think that is quite enough to condemn the steamer. "

"Undoubtedly; but what is the Ionian to do in the Bermudas? That is what perplexes me, " said the detective.

"Possibly Captain Chantor can solve the problem, for I am sure I cannot, " answered the young officer, as he rose from his seat.

He was as much perplexed as his companion, and he went on deck to wait the appearance of the commander. About nine o'clock he came upon the quarter-deck. The Ionian remained at the same relative distance from the Chateaugay, for the captain had given an order to this effect before he turned in.

"I am glad to see you, Captain Chantor, " said Christy. "Can you explain why the Ionian is headed for the Bermudas, for you have later information than any in my possession? "

"I think I can, " replied the captain, taking a letter from his pocket. "This is the contents of the last envelope brought off from the shore. The writer of it says he has just addressed a letter to 'our friend in New York, ' directing him, if it is not too late, to send the steamer with the machinery and other merchandise to the Bermudas, where the cargo will be transferred to the Dornoch; for the Ovidio had been obliged to sail without her armament, and the cargo was too valuable to be risked without protection. "

"That is the reason why the reinforcement was sent off at the last moment, " Christy remarked.

"The Dornoch carries six guns and fifty men, " added the captain, reading from the letter. "I think we need not wait any longer to take possession of the Ionian, Mr. Passford. What is your opinion? "

"I concur entirely with you, " replied Christy.

"Quartermaster, strike four bells, " continued the captain to the man who was conning the wheel.

"Four bells, " repeated the quartermaster; and the gong could be heard on deck as he did so.

In the course of half an hour, for the steam had been kept rather low for the slow progress the ship was obliged to make in order not to alarm the chase, the Chateaugay began to show what she could do in the matter of speed, and before noon she had overhauled the Ionian.

CHAPTER VI

THE BOARDING OF THE IONIAN

The Chateaugay, with her colors flying, ran abreast of the Ionian and by her; but the latter did not show her flag. A blank cartridge was then fired, but the steamer took no notice of it. A shot was then discharged across her fore foot, and this brought her to her senses, so that she hoisted the British flag, and stopped her screw. All the preparations had been made for boarding her, and two boats were in readiness to discharge this duty.

The first cutter, in charge of Mr. Birdwing, was the first to leave the ship. The sea was quite smooth, so that there was no difficulty in getting the boats off. The first lieutenant's boat went from the starboard side, and the second cutter was lowered on the port in charge of the third lieutenant. Christy went in the first boat, and Mr. Gilfleur in the second. The officers and crews of both boats were especially directed to see that nothing was thrown overboard from the Ionian; for if her captain found that he was in a "tight place, " he would be likely to heave his papers into the sea.

The first cutter had not made half the distance to the Ionian before she pulled down the British flag and hoisted the American in its place. Her commander evidently believed that he was getting into hot water, and well he might. He must have been selected for this enterprise on account of his fitness for it, and as the steamer had not sailed on an honest voyage, he could not be an honest man, and the officers of the boats despised him. They were determined to discharge their duty faithfully, even if they were obliged to treat him with the utmost rigor.

"She has corrected her first blunder, " said Mr. Birdwing, as the American flag went up to her peak. "The skipper of that craft don't exactly know what he is about. "

"It must be a surprise to him to be brought to by a United States man-of-war, " added Christy.

"But why did the fool hoist the British flag when he has no papers to back it up? That would have done very well among the blockaders, " continued the officer of the boat. "I don't know very much about this business, and the captain ordered me to let you and the French gentleman in the other boat have your own way on board of her, and to do all you required. Have you any directions for me?"

"We desire to have the steamer thoroughly searched, and I have little doubt that we shall ask you to take possession of her," replied Christy.

"Then we are to make a capture of it?" asked the first lieutenant, manifesting no little surprise.

"Under certain circumstances, yes."

"Is she a Confederate vessel?"

"No; she is an American vessel."

"All right; but I shall obey my orders to the very letter," added Mr. Birdwing. "How many men shall I put on board of her?"

"Twelve, if you please," replied Christy, who had arranged the plan with the detective.

"Six from each boat," said the executive officer; and then he hailed the second cutter, and directed Mr. Carlin to send this number on board of the Ionian.

"And, if you please, direct him to board the steamer on the starboard side, for I take it you will board on the port," added Christy. "We fear that she will throw certain papers overboard, and we must prevent that if possible."

The order was given to the third lieutenant, and in a few minutes more the first cutter came alongside the steamer. Mr. Birdwing ordered those on board to drop the accommodation ladder over the side; and for so mild a gentleman he did it in a very imperative tone. The order was obeyed, though it appeared to be done very reluctantly. The first lieutenant was the first to mount the ladder, and was closely followed by his passenger.

"Where is the captain?" demanded Mr. Birdwing, as the six men detailed for the purpose were coming over the side.

"I am the captain, " replied an ill-favored looking man, stepping forward with very ill grace.

"What steamer is this? "

"The Ionian, of New York, bound to St. George's, Bermuda, " replied the captain in a crusty tone.

"The captain's name? " demanded the officer, becoming more imperative as the commander of the Ionian manifested more of his crabbed disposition.

"Captain Sawlock, " growled the ill-favored master of the steamer, who was a rather short man, thick-set, with a face badly pitted by the small-pox, but nearly covered with a grizzly and tangled beard.

"You will oblige me by producing your papers, Captain Sawlock, " continued Mr. Birdwing.

"For a good reason, my papers are not regular, " answered the captain of the Ionian, with an attempt to be more affable, though it did not seem to be in his nature to be anything but a brute in his manners.

"Regular or not, you will oblige me by exhibiting them, " the officer insisted.

"It is not my fault that a change was made in my orders after I got under way, " pleaded Captain Sawlock.

"Will you produce your clearance and other papers? " demanded the lieutenant very decidedly.

"This is an American vessel, and you have no right to overhaul me in this manner, " growled the captain of the steamer.

"You are in command of a steamer, and you cannot be so ignorant as to believe that an officer of a man-of-war has not the right to require you to show your papers, " added Mr. Birdwing with a palpable sneer.

"This is an American vessel, " repeated Captain Sawlock.

"Then why did you hoist the British flag? "

"That's my business! "

"But it is mine also. Do you decline to show your papers? You are trifling with me, " said Mr. Birdwing impatiently.

At this moment there was a scuffle in the waist of the steamer, which attracted the attention of all on the deck. Mr. Gilfleur had suddenly thrown himself on the first officer of the Ionian; and when his second officer and several sailors had gone to his assistance, the third lieutenant of the Chateaugay had rushed in to the support of the Frenchman. The man-of-war's men were all armed with cutlasses and revolvers; but they did not use their weapons, and it looked like a rough-and-tumble fight on the deck.

Mr. Birdwing and Christy rushed over to the starboard side of the steamer; but Mr. Carlin and his men had so effectively sustained the detective that the affray had reached a conclusion before they could interfere. Mr. Gilfleur was crawling out from under two or three men who had thrown themselves upon him when he brought the first officer to the deck by jumping suddenly upon him. The Frenchman had in his hand a tin case about a foot in length, and three inches in diameter, such as are sometimes used to contain charters, or similar valuable papers.

The contest had plainly been for the possession of this case, which the quick eye of the detective had discovered as the mate was carrying it forward; for Mr. Carlin had sent two of his men to the stern at the request of the Frenchman, charged to allow no one to throw anything overboard. The first officer of the Ionian had listened to the conversation between Captain Sawlock and the first lieutenant, and had gone below into the cabin when it began to be a little stormy.

"What does all this mean, Mr. Carlin? " inquired Mr. Birdwing.

"I simply obeyed my orders to support Mr. Gilfleur; and he can explain his action better than I can, " replied the third lieutenant.

"I have requested the officers, through Captain Chantor, to see that nothing was thrown overboard, either before or after we boarded the steamer, " interposed Christy.

Fighting for the Right

"And the captain's order has been obeyed, " added the first lieutenant. "Will you explain the cause of this affray, Mr. Gilfleur? "

"With the greatest pleasure, " answered the detective with one of his politest bows. "While you were talking with the captain of the Ionian, I saw the first officer of this steamer go into the cabin. I was told by a sailor that he was the mate. In a minute or two he came on deck again, and I saw that he had something under his coat. He moved forward, and was going to the side when I jumped upon him. After a struggle I took this tin case from him. "

The detective stepped forward, and handed the tin case to the executive officer as gracefully as though he had been figuring in a ballroom. Captain Sawlock had followed the officers over from the port side. He appeared to be confounded, and listened in silence to the explanation of Mr. Gilfleur. But he looked decidedly ugly.

"That case is my personal, private property, " said he, as soon as it was in the hands of the chief officer of the boarding-party.

"I don't dispute it, Captain Sawlock; but at the same time I intend to examine its contents, " replied Mr. Birdwing mildly, but firmly.

"This is an outrage, Mr. Officer! " exclaimed the discomfited master.

"If it is, I am responsible for it, " added the executive officer, as he removed the cover from the end of the case.

"I protest against this outrage! I will not submit to it! " howled Captain Sawlock, carried away by his wrath.

"Perhaps you will, " said Mr. Birdwing quietly.

"But I will not! "

With a sudden movement he threw himself upon the officer, and attempted to wrest the tin case from his hands. Christy, who was standing behind him, seized him by the collar with both hands, and hurled him to the deck. A moment later two seamen, by order of Mr. Carlin, took him each by his two arms, and held him like a vice.

"I think we will retire to the cabin to examine these papers, for I see that the case is filled with documents, including some sealed letters," continued Mr. Birdwing, as he moved towards the cabin door.

"That cabin is mine! You can't go into it! " howled Captain Sawlock, crazy with anger. "Don't let them go into the cabin, Withers! "

Withers appeared to be the mate, and he stepped forward as though he intended to do something; but a couple of seamen, by order of the first lieutenant, arrested and held him. He had apparently had enough of it in his encounter with the detective, for he submitted without any resistance. If the captain of the steamer was a fool, the mate was not, for he saw the folly of resisting a United States force.

"Mr. Carlin, you will remain on deck with the men; Mr. Passford and Mr. Gilfleur, may I trouble you to come into the cabin with me? " continued Mr. Birdwing, as he led the way.

The executive officer seated himself at the table in the middle of the cabin, and his companions took places on each side of him. The first paper drawn from the case was the clearance of the Ionian for Wilmington, with a cargo of old iron. The manifest had clearly been trumped up for the occasion. The old iron was specified, and a list of other articles of merchandise.

At this point the executive officer sent for Mr. Carlin, and directed him to take off the hatches and examine the cargo, especially what was under the pieces of machinery. There were several letters to unknown persons, and one in particular to the captain himself, in which he was directed to deliver the machinery to a gentleman with the title of "Captain, " who was doubtless a Confederate agent, in St. George's, Bermuda. The papers were abundantly sufficient to convict Davis of treason. The last one found in the case directed Captain Sawlock to deliver the cannon and ammunition in the bottom of the vessel to the steamer Dornoch, on her arrival at St. George's, or at some convenient place in the Bahama Islands.

CHAPTER VII

A BOLD PROPOSITION

The evidence was sufficient to justify the capture of the Ionian without a particle of doubt, for she was as really a Confederate vessel as though the captain and officers were provided with commissions signed by Mr. Jefferson Davis.

Mr. Birdwing went to the door and directed the third lieutenant to have Captain Sawlock conducted to the cabin; and the two seamen who had held him as a prisoner brought him before the first lieutenant of the Chateaugay. He appeared to have got control of his temper, and offered no further resistance. Mr. Carlin came to the door, and his superior directed him to examine all hands forward, in order to ascertain whether they were Confederates or otherwise. He gave him the shipping-list to assist him.

"Are you an American citizen, Captain Sawlock? " asked Mr. Birdwing, as soon as the third lieutenant had departed on his mission.

"I am, " replied he stiffly.

"Where were you horn? "

"In Pensacola. "

"Have you ever taken the oath of allegiance to the United States government? "

"No; and I never will! " protested the captain with an oath.

"I must inform you, Captain Sawlock, that I am directed by the commander of the United States steamer Chateaugay to take possession of the Ionian, on finding sufficient evidence on board that she is engaged in an illegal voyage. I have no doubt in regard to the matter, and I take possession of her accordingly. "

"It is an outrage! " howled the captain with a heavy oath.

"You can settle that matter with the courts. I have nothing more to say, " replied Mr. Birdwing as he rose and left the cabin, followed by Christy and the detective.

"I found ten heavy guns and a large quantity of ammunition at the bottom of the hold, " reported Mr. Carlin, as his superior appeared on deck, and handed back the shipping-list of the vessel. "The three engineers appear to be Englishmen, and so declare themselves. I find six Americans among the crew, who are provided with protections, and they all desire to enlist in the navy. The rest of the crew are of all nations. "

"Let the six men with protections man the first cutter. You will remain on board of the Ionian, Mr. Carlin, till orders come to you from the captain, " said the first lieutenant. "I shall now return to the Chateaugay to report. "

Christy decided to return to the ship; but the detective wished to remain, though he said there was nothing more for him to do. The six sailors who wished to enter the navy were ordered into the boat, two of the regular crew remaining in it. The recruits were good-looking men, and they pulled their oars as though they had already served in the navy. They supposed the Ionian was really bound to Wilmington; but they could not explain why they had not enlisted at Brooklyn if they desired to do so. The first lieutenant went on board of the ship, and reported to the captain.

Mr. Gwyndale was at once appointed prize-master, with Mr. Tompers as his executive officer, and sent on board with the ten seamen who had been put on board of the Chateaugay expressly for this duty. Several pairs of handcuffs were sent on board of the Ionian, for the first lieutenant apprehended that they would be needed to keep Captain Sawlock and his mate in proper subjection. The papers which had been contained in the tin case were intrusted to the care of Mr. Gwyndale, with the strictest injunction to keep them safely, and deliver them to the government official before any of the Ionian ship's company were permitted to land.

The cutters returned from the prize with all the hands who had been sent from the ship, including Mr. Gilfleur. The prize-master had a sufficient force with him to handle the steamer, and to control the disaffected, if there were any besides the captain and mate. The engineers and firemen were willing to remain and do duty as long as they were paid. In a couple of hours the Ionian started her screw and headed for New York, where she would arrive the next day.

Captain Chantor directed the quartermaster at the wheel to ring one bell, and the Chateaugay began to move again. The events of the day were discussed; but the first business of the ship had been successfully disposed of, and the future was a more inviting field than the past. The captain requested the presence of the two passengers in his cabin, and read to them in full the latest instructions that had been sent off to him.

"Our next duty is to look for the Dornoch, with her six guns and fifty men, and we are not likely to have so soft a time of it as we had with the Ionian," said Captain Chantor, when he had read the letter.

"The Chateaugay is reasonably fast, though she could not hold her own with the Bellevite, or even the Bronx; and you have a pivot gun amidships, and six broadside guns," added Christy.

"Oh, I shall be happy to meet her!" exclaimed the commander. "I don't object to her six guns and fifty men; the only difficulty I can see is in finding her. I am afraid she has already gone into St. George's harbor, and she may not come out for a month."

"Why should she wait all that time?" asked Christy. "Her commander knew nothing about the Ionian, that she was to take in a valuable cargo for her, and she will not wait for her."

"That is true; but I am afraid we shall miss the Ovidio if we remain too long in these waters."

"It seems to me that the Dornoch has had time enough to reach the Bermudas," said Christy. "Possibly she is in port at this moment."

"That is a harassing reflection!" exclaimed the commander.

"I don't see that there is any help for it," added Christy. "You cannot go into the port of St. George's to see if she is there."

"Why not?" asked Mr. Gilfleur, speaking for the first time. "I spent a winter there when I was sick from over-work and exposure; and I know all about the islands."

"That will not help me, Mr. Gilfleur, " said the captain, with a smile at what he considered the simplicity of the Frenchman.

"But why can you not go in and see if the Dornoch is there? " inquired the detective.

"Because if I learned that she was about to leave the port, the authorities would not let me sail till twenty-four hours after she had gone. "

"You need not wait till she gets ready to leave, " suggested the Frenchman.

"She might be ready to sail at the very time I arrived, and then I should lose her. Oh, no; I prefer to take my chance at a marine league from the shore, " added the captain, shaking his head.

"Perhaps I might go into Hamilton harbor and obtain the information you need, " suggested Mr. Gilfleur, looking very earnest, as though he was thinking of something.

"You! " exclaimed Captain Chantor, looking at him with amazement. "How could you go in without going in the ship? "

"You know that I have a boat on deck, " replied the detective quietly.

"But you are not a sailor, sir. "

"No, I am not a sailor; but I am a boatman. After I had worked up the biggest case in all my life in Paris, —one that required me to go to London seven times, —I was sick when the bank-robbers were convicted, and the excitement was over. The doctors ordered me to spend the winter in Martinique, and I went to the Bermudas in an English steamer, where I was to take another for my destination; but I liked the islands so well that I remained there all the winter. My principal amusement was boating; and I learned the whole art to perfection. I used to go through the openings in the reefs, and sail out of sight of land. I had a boat like the one on deck. "

"Your experience is interesting, but I do not see how it will profit me," said the captain.

"I can go to the Bermudas, obtain the information you want, and return to the Chateaugay," replied Mr. Gilfleur rather impatiently.

"That would be a risky cruise for you, my friend," suggested Captain Chantor, shaking his head in a deprecatory manner.

"I don't think so. I have been outside the reefs many times when the wind blew a gale, and I felt as safe in my boat as I do on board of this ship," said the detective earnestly.

"How would you manage the matter?" asked the commander, beginning to be interested in the project.

"You shall run to the south of the islands, or rather to the south-west, in the night, with all your lights put out, and let me embark there in my boat. You will give me a compass, and I have a sail in the boat. I shall steer to the north-east, and I shall soon see Gibbs Hill light. By that I can make the point on the coast I wish to reach, which is Hogfish Cut. I have been through it twenty times. Once inside the reefs I shall have no difficulty in reaching Hamilton harbor. Then I will take a carriage to St. George's. If I find the Dornoch in the harbor, I will come out the same way I went in, and you will pick me up."

"That looks more practicable than I supposed it could be," added Captain Chantor.

"While I am absent you will be attending to your duty as commander of the Chateaugay, for you will still be on the lookout for your prize," continued the versatile Frenchman. "You can run up twenty or thirty miles to the northward, on the east side of the islands, where all large vessels have to go in."

"How long will it take you to carry out this enterprise, Mr. Gilfleur?"

"Not more than two days; perhaps less time. Do you consent?"

"I will consider it, and give you an answer to-morrow morning," replied Captain Chantor.

"Won't you take me with you, Mr. Gilfleur?" asked Christy, who was much pleased with the idea of such an excursion.

"I should be very happy to have your company, Mr. Passford," replied the detective very promptly, and with a smile on his face which revealed his own satisfaction.

"Are you in earnest, Lieutenant Passford?" demanded the commander, looking with astonishment at his passenger.

"Of course I am: I see no difficulty in the enterprise," replied Christy. "I have had a good deal of experience in sailboats myself, and I do not believe I should be an encumbrance to Mr. Gilfleur; and I may be of some service to him."

"You would be of very great service to me, for you know all about ships, and I do not," the detective added.

"Just as you please, Mr. Passford. You are not under my orders, for you are not attached to the ship," said the captain.

The commander went on deck, and the two passengers retired to Christy's stateroom, where they discussed the enterprise for a couple of hours. In the mean time the Chateaugay was making her best speed, for Captain Chantor did not wish to lose any of his chances by being too late; and he believed that the Dornoch must be fully due at the Bermudas. Before he turned in that night he had altered the course of the ship half a point more to the southward, for he had decided to accept the offer of Mr. Gilfleur; and he wished to go to the west of the islands instead of the east, as he had given out the course at noon.

For two days more the Chateaugay continued on her voyage. At noon the second day he found his ship was directly west of the southern part of the Bermudas, and but fifty miles from them. He shaped his course so as to be at the south of them that night.

CHAPTER VIII

A NOTABLE EXPEDITION

The position of the Chateaugay was accurately laid down on the chart fifty miles to the westward of Spears Hill, which is about the geographical centre of the Bermuda Islands. Captain Chantor had invited his two passengers to his cabin for a conference in relation to the proposed enterprise, after the observations had been worked up at noon, on the fourth day after the departure from New York.

"Now, Mr. Gilfleur, if you will indicate the precise point at which you desire to put off in your boat, I will have the ship there at the time you require, " said the captain, who had drawn a rough sketch of the islands, and dotted upon it the points he mentioned in his statement.

"Of course you do not wish the ship to be seen from the islands, " suggested the detective.

"Certainly not; for if the Dornoch is in port at St. George's that would be warning her to avoid us in coming out, and she might escape by standing off to the northward, " replied the commander. "Besides, there might be fishing-craft or other small vessels off the island that would report the ship if she were seen. It is not advisable to go any nearer to the islands till after dark. We will show no lights as we approach your destination. "

"How near Gibbs Hill light can you go with safety in the darkness, Captain? " asked Mr. Gilfleur.

"I should not care to go nearer than ten miles; we could not be seen from the shore at that distance, but we might be seen by some small craft. "

"That will do very well; and if you will make a point ten miles southwest of Gibbs Hills light, I shall be exactly suited, " added the detective, as he made a small cross on the sketch near the place where he desired to embark in the boat.

The conference was finished, and the two passengers went on deck to inspect the craft which was to convey them to the islands. By order of the commander the carpenter had overhauled the boat and made such repairs as were needed. Every open seam had been calked, and a heavy coat of paint had been put upon it. The sailmaker had attended to the jib and mainsail, and everything was in excellent condition for the trip to the shore.

"Is this the same boat that you used when you were in the Bermudas, Mr. Gilfleur?" asked Christy, as they were examining the work which had been done on the craft, its spars and sails.

"Oh, no; it was six years ago that I spent the winter in the islands. I found this boat under a shed on a wharf in New York. It had been picked up near the Great Abaco in the Bahama Islands by a three-master, on her voyage from the West Indies," replied Mr. Gilfleur. "When I had formed my plan of operations in the vicinity of Nassau, in order to obtain the information the government desired, I bought this boat. When picked up, the boat had her spars, sails, oars, water-breakers, and other articles carefully stowed away on board of her; and it appeared as though she had broken adrift from her moorings, or had been carried away by a rising tide from some beach where those in charge of her had landed. I happened to find the captain of the vessel that brought the boat to New York; and he made me pay roundly for her, so that he got well rewarded for his trouble in picking it up."

The Chateaugay stood due south till six o'clock at little more than half speed, and when she came about her dead reckoning indicated that she was seventy-five miles to the south-west of Gibbs Hill light. The weather was very favorable for the proposed enterprise, with a moderate breeze from the west. Mr. Gilfleur did not wish to leave the ship till after midnight, for all he desired was to get inside the outer reefs before daylight. The speed of the ship was regulated to carry out this idea.

The light so frequently mentioned in the conference is three hundred and sixty-two feet above the sea level, for it is built on the highest point of land in the south of the Bermudas, and could be seen at a distance of thirty miles. At three bells in the first watch the light was reported by the lookout, and the speed was reduced somewhat.

About this time the detective came out of his stateroom, and entered that of Christy. He had smeared his face with a brownish tint, which made him look as though he had been long exposed to the sun of the tropics. He was dressed in a suit of coarse material, though it was not the garb of a sailor. He had used the scissors on his long black mustache, and given it a snarly and unkempt appearance. Christy would not have known him if he had met him on shore.

"You look like another man, " said he, laughing.

"A French detective has to learn the art of disguising himself; in fact, he has to be an actor. Perhaps you will not be willing to believe it, but I have played small parts at the Théâtre Français for over a year, more to learn the actor's art of making himself up than because I had any histrionic aspirations. I have worked up a case in the capacity of an old man of eighty years of age, " the detective explained. "When I recovered the property of your father, stolen at Havre, I played the part of a dandy, and won the confidence of the stewardess, though I came very near having to fight a duel with the *voleur* who was her 'pal' in the robbery. "

"Of course it will not do for me to wear my lieutenant's uniform, " suggested Christy.

"Not unless you wish to have your head broken by the crews of the blockade-runners you will find at St. George's, " replied the Frenchman significantly.

"I have some old clothes in my valise, " added the lieutenant.

"I don't like the idea of putting you in a humiliating position, Mr. Passford, but I have not told you all my plans. "

"I will take any position you assign to me, for I am now to be a volunteer in your service. "

"I intend to represent myself as a French gentleman of wealth, who has passed the winter in the Bahama Islands in search of health, and found it in abundance, " said Mr. Gilfleur, with a pleasant smile on his face, as though he really enjoyed the business in which he was at present engaged.

"Have you ever been in the Bahamas? " asked Christy.

"All through them, including Nassau. If I had not, I should not have brought that boat with me. I made a trip in an English steamer from the Bermudas, which had occasion to visit nearly all the islands; and I passed about two months of my stay in this region on that cruise, " replied the detective.

"But how far is it from the Bermudas to the nearest point in the Bahamas? Will people believe that we came even from the Great Abaco in an open boat? " inquired Christy. "What is the distance? "

"I estimate it at about seven hundred and fifty miles. That is nothing for a boat like mine, though I should not care to undertake it in the hurricane season, " replied Mr. Gilfleur. "By the way, we must borrow some charts of this region from the captain, though only to keep up appearances. "

"You have not told me in what character I am to be your companion," suggested Christy.

"As my servant, if you do not rebel at the humiliation of such a position, though I promise to treat you very kindly, and with all proper consideration, " laughed the Frenchman.

"I have not the slightest objection to the character; and I will endeavor to discharge my duties with humility and deference, " responded the lieutenant in the same vein.

"Now let me see what sort of a suit you have for your part, " added the detective.

Christy took from his valise a suit he had worn as a subordinate officer when he was engaged in the capture of the Teaser. It was approved by his companion, and he dressed himself in this garb.

"But you have been bleached out by your long stay at Bonnydale, and your complexion needs a little improvement, " said Mr. Gilfleur, as he went to his room for his tints.

On his return he gave to the face of the officer the same sun-browned hue he had imparted to his own. While he was so employed, he explained that the tint was a fast color under ordinary circumstances, and in what manner it could be easily removed, though it would wear off in about a week.

"Now, you need only a little touching up," continued the detective, when he had completed the dyeing process. "You will be amazed at the change produced in the expression of a person by a few touches of paint skilfully applied," and he proceeded to make the alteration proposed.

When he had finished his work, Christy looked in the glass, and declared that he should hardly know himself. The preparations were completed, and the French gentleman and his servant were ready to embark. But it was only eleven o'clock, and both of them turned in for a nap of a couple of hours. The captain had retired early in the evening, and the quartermaster conning the wheel was steering for the light, the Chateaugay making not more than six knots an hour.

At one o'clock the commander was called, in accordance with his order to the officer of the watch. He went on deck at once, had the log slate brought to him, and made some calculations, which resulted in an order to ring two bells, which meant "Stop her." Then he went to the ward room himself, and knocked at the doors of his two passengers. Mr. Gilfleur and Christy sprang from their berths, and the two doors were opened at once. No toilet was necessary, for both of them had lain down with their clothes on.

"Pray, who might you be?" demanded the captain, laughing heartily when the detective showed himself in his new visage and dress. "Can you inform me what has become of Mr. Gilfleur?"

"He has stepped out for a couple of days, and Monsieur Rubempré has taken his place," replied the detective.

"And who is this gentleman?" asked Captain Chantor, turning to his other passenger, who was quite as much changed in appearance.

"Contrary to his usual custom, he does not claim to be a gentleman just now. This is Christophe, my servant, employed as such only for a couple of days," answered Monsieur Rubempré.

"All right, Mr. Rubumper! Three bells have just been struck, and the watch are putting your boat into the water," continued the commander. "I have directed the steward to fill your breaker with water, and put a small supply of provisions into the craft. We shall be ready for you in about half an hour."

"We are all ready at this moment, " replied Monsieur Rubempré; for both of the passengers had agreed to call each other by their assumed names at once, so as to get accustomed to them, and thus avoid committing themselves in any moment of excitement.

The detective came out of his room with a valise in his hand, which he had packed with extreme care, so that nothing should be found in it, in case of accident, to compromise him. He had superintended the placing of Christy's clothing in one of his valises. He objected to the initials, "C. P., " worked on his linen; but the owner had no other, and the difficulty was compromised by writing the name of "Christophe Poireau" on a number of pieces of paper and cards, and attaching a tag with this name upon it to the handle.

Both of them put on plain overcoats, and went on deck, where the boat, which had the name of Eleuthera painted on the stern, had already been committed to the waves.

CHAPTER IX

THE FRENCHMAN IN BERMUDA

"Bon voyage, Mr. Rubumper, " said Captain Chanter, as the Frenchman was about to descend the accommodation ladder. "I know French enough to say that. "

"Thank you, Captain. "

"I hope you will make a success of the enterprise, Mr. Passford, " the commander added to the other member of the expedition.

"I shall do the best I can to make it so, " answered Christy, as he followed his companion down the accommodation ladder.

The detective shoved the boat off, and both of the voyagers took the oars to get the craft clear of the ship, which was accomplished in a few minutes. Then the Frenchman stepped the mast, which had been carefully adjusted on board of the ship, while Christy rigged out the shifting bowsprit. In half an hour they had placed the spars and bent on the sail, for everything had been prepared for expeditious work. The sails filled, and the skipper took his place at the long tiller.

"We are all right now, Christophe, " said the detective.

"I should say that we were, Monsieur Rubempré, " replied the acting servant. "We have ten miles to make: with this breeze, how long will it take for this boat to do it? "

"If she sails as well as mine did, she will make it in two hours. "

The craft was about twenty feet long, and was sharp at both ends. She had a cuddy forward, which was large enough to accommodate both of her crew in a reclining posture. It had been furnished with a couple of berthsacks, and with several blankets. The provisions and water had been placed in it, as well as a couple of lanterns, ready for use if occasion should require.

It was a summer sea in this latitude, with a very steady breeze from the westward. The overcoats they wore were hardly necessary, and they had put them on mainly to conceal their changed garments from the crew of the ship, who could only conjecture what the expedition meant.

"You are a younger man than I am, Christophe, and you have slept only a couple of hours to-night, " said M. Rubempré, as soon as the Eleuthera was well under way; and the remark was called forth by a long gape on the part of the younger person. "You can turn in and sleep a couple of hours more just as well as not, for there is nothing whatever for you to do. We may have to make a long day of it to-morrow. "

"I am accustomed to doing without my sleep at times, " replied Christophe, which was his first name, according to the French orthography, and was pronounced in two syllables.

"Of course you have, when your duty required you to be on deck; but there is not the least need of doing so now. "

The lieutenant complied with the advice of the skipper, and in five minutes more he was sound asleep. The Bahama boat, with a Bahama name, rose and fell on the long rolling seas, which were very gentle in their motion, and made very good progress through the water. The light could be plainly seen in its lofty position, and the detective steered for it over an hour, and then kept it a little on the starboard hand; for the opening in the outer reef through which he intended to pass was two miles to the westward of the high tower. He had correctly estimated the speed of the boat, for the faint light of the dawn of day began to appear in the east when he was able clearly to discern the outline of the hills on the most southern of the islands.

Although it was still quite dark, the Frenchman continued on his course very confidently. The reefs extended out two miles from the main shore; but the navigator was so familiar with the locality that they did not trouble him. Bearing about north-west from the light was Wreck Hill, one hundred and fifty feet high, which assisted him in keeping his course. As he approached the mainland he made out the fort, and steering directly for it, passed safely through Hogfish Cut.

When he was within half a mile of this fort, he headed the boat to the north-west. It was still eighteen miles to Hamilton, the capital of the islands; but he had a fair wind, and the boat made about five miles an hour. Christy still slept, and the skipper did not wake him. It was daylight when he was abreast of Wreck Hill, and there was no further difficulty in the navigation. It was half-past eight when he ran up to a pier where he had kept his boat in former days. There were plenty of just such crafts as the Eleuthera, and no attention was paid to her as she passed along the Front-street docks. The pier at which he made his landing was in a retired locality. He lowered the sails, and had made everything snug on board before he called his companion.

"Half-past eight, Christophe, " said he at the door of the cuddy.

"Half-past eight! " exclaimed Christy, springing out of his berth on the floor. "Where are we now, M. Rubempré? "

"We are in Hamilton harbor; and if you will come out of the cuddy, you will find yourself in the midst of flowers and green trees, " replied the skipper with a smile.

"I must have slept six hours, " said Christy, rubbing his eyes as he crawled out of the cuddy.

The scenery around him was certainly very beautiful, and he gazed upon it in silence for a few minutes. It seemed to him just as though he had waked in fairyland. He had cruised in the vicinity of the islands, but he had never been very near the shore before. Though he had been in Alabama, and seen the shores of the Gulf States, he had never beheld any region that seemed so lovely to him. He had been on shore at Nassau, but only on the wharves, and had hardly seen the beauties of the island.

"Why didn't you call me before, M. Rubempré? " asked he, when he had taken in the view from the pier.

"Because I thought your sleep would do you more good than the view of the shore, which you will have plenty of opportunities to see before we leave, " replied the detective. "But we must begin our work, for we have no time to lose. I arranged with Captain Chantor to pick us up to-morrow night at about the point where we embarked in the boat. In the mean time he will sail around the islands, though the Chateaugay will not come near enough to be seen from the shore. "

Fighting for the Right

"What will you do with the boat while we are absent? "

"Leave it where it is. "

While they were talking, an old negro came down the pier, and very politely saluted the strangers. He appeared to come from a small house a short distance from the shore, and passed along to a boat which lay near the Eleuthera.

"Is that your boat? " asked the detective, calling him back.

"Yes, sir; I am a fisherman, though I've got the rheumatism, and don't go out much; but I have to go to-day, for we have nothing to eat in the house, " replied the negro, whose language was very good.

"What is your name? "

"Joseph, sir. "

"Do you speak French? "

"Oh, no, sir! " exclaimed Joseph. "I don't speak anything but plain English; but I used to work sometimes for a French gentleman that kept a boat at this pier, six or seven years ago. "

"What was his came? " asked the detective, who had had a suspicion from the first that he knew the man, though he had changed a great deal as he grew older.

"Mounseer Gillflower, " replied Joseph; "and he was very kind to me. "

"I am a Frenchman, Joseph; and, if you don't want to go fishing, I will employ you to take care of my boat, and carry my valise to a hotel, " continued the detective, as he handed an English sovereign to him, for he had taken care to provide himself with a store of them in New York.

"Thank you, sir; but I can't change this piece, " protested Joseph very sadly.

"I don't want you to change it; keep the whole of it. "

"God bless you forever and ever, Mounseer!" exclaimed the fisherman. "I haven't had a sovereign before since Mounseer Gillflower was here. I am a very poor man, and I can't get any work on shore."

Probably, like the rest of his class, he was not inclined to work while he had any money. He promised to take good care of the Eleuthera, and he asked no troublesome questions. The detective gave his name, and ordered Christophe, calling him by his name, to bring the valises on shore. Then the Frenchman locked the door of the cuddy, for they left their overcoats there, as they had no use for them.

"To what hotel shall I carry the valises?" asked Joseph.

"To the Atlantic; that will be the most convenient for us. Do you know anything about these vessels in the harbor, Joseph?"

"Not much, Mounseer Roobump; but they say the two steamers near the island are going to run the blockade into the States; but I don't know. They say a Confederate man-of-war came into St. George's harbor yesterday; but I haven't seen her, and I don't know whether it's true or not."

"What is her name?" asked the detective, who from the beginning had broken up his English, and imparted a strong French accent to it.

"I did not hear any one mention her name, Mounseer. That vessel this side of the island is the mail steamer from New York; she got in yesterday," continued Joseph.

"That is important; if the Dornoch is the Confederate man-of-war that arrived at St. George's yesterday, this steamer brought letters from Davis to her captain," said the Frenchman to Christy, in French.

"But Davis could not have learned that the Ionian had been captured before the mail steamer left New York," added Christy, in the same language.

"No matter for that, Christophe. I did not resign my place at Davis's warehouse till the morning we sailed; and I have his letter to the captain of the Dornoch with my other papers on board of the Chateaugay, and I know that was the only letter written to him. As he has no information in regard to the Ionian, he will not wait for her."

"I remember; you showed me the letter."

Joseph listened with a show of wonder on his face to this conversation which he could not understand. The detective directed him to carry the two valises to the hotel named; but Christy interposed in French, and insisted that it would look better for him to carry his own valise, and the point was yielded. The Atlantic Hotel was on Front Street, the harbor being on one side of it. A couple of rooms were assigned to them, one of them quite small, which was taken by Christy, in order to keep up appearances.

M. Rubempré registered his name, putting "and servant" after it, Paris, and spoke even worse English than he had used to Joseph. Breakfast had been ordered, but Christy, being only a servant, had to take his meal at a side table. The detective was not dressed like a gentleman, and the landlord seemed to have some doubts about his ability to pay his bills, though he had baggage. He was not treated with anything like deference, and he saw the difficulty. After breakfast he took a handful of English gold from his pocket, and asked the landlord to change one of the coins for smaller money. Mine host bowed low to him after this exhibition.

"I want to see the American consul," said M. Rubempré, in his own language.

"I will go with you, but I think I will not see him, for he may take it into his head that I am not a Frenchman," added Christy.

"You can come with me, and stay outside."

When they reached the consulate, which was on the same street as the hotel, they found about a dozen sailors in front of the building. They were a very rough and hard-looking set of men. They appeared to be considerably excited about something, and to be bent on violence in some direction; but the strangers could make nothing of the talk they heard, though "the bloody spy" was an expression frequently used.

CHAPTER X

IMPORTANT INFORMATION OBTAINED

Christy walked behind the detective in his capacity as servant. It was soon evident to them that the ruffians gathered in the street meant mischief. On the staff over their heads floated the flag of the United States. Though Mr. Gilfleur was an alien, his companion was not. Of course he knew that the islands were the resort of blockade-runners, that they obtained their supplies from the two towns of Hamilton and St. George's. This fact seemed to explain the occasion of the disturbance in this particular locality.

"What does all this mean, Christophe? " asked M. Rubempré, falling back to join Christy at the door of the consulate.

"I should judge that these ruffians intended to do violence to the American consul, " replied Christy. "I heard in New York that he was faithful in the discharge of his duty to his government, and doubtless he has excited the indignation of these ruffians by his fidelity. His principal business is to follow up the enforcement of the neutrality laws, which compels him to watch these blockade-runners, and vessels of war intended for the Confederate States. "

"That was my own conclusion, " added the Frenchman, speaking his own language, as usual. "I should say that his position is not a pleasant one. "

"Here comes the bloody spy! " shouted several of the ruffians.

Looking down the street, they saw a dignified-looking gentleman approaching, whom they supposed to be the consul, Mr. Alwayn. He did not seem to be alarmed at the demonstration in front of his office. The disturbers of the peace fell back as he advanced, and he reached the door where the detective and his companion were standing without being attacked. The mob, now considerably increased in numbers, though probably more than a majority, as usual, were merely spectators, hooted violently at the representative of the United States.

The gentleman reached the door of his office, and by this time the ruffians seemed to realize that simple hooting did no harm, and they rushed forward with more serious intentions. One of them laid violent hands on the consul, seizing him by the back of his coat collar, and attempting to pull him over backwards. Christy felt that he was under the flag of his country, and his blood boiled with indignation; and, rash as was the act, he planted a heavy blow with his fist under the ear of the assailant, which sent him reeling back among his companions.

"No revolvers, Christophe! " said the detective earnestly, as he placed himself by the side of the young man.

Christy's revolver was in his hip-pocket, where he usually carried it, and the detective feared he might use it, for both of them could hardly withstand the pressure upon them; and the firing of a single shot would have roused the passions of the mob, and led to no little bloodshed. M. Rubempré was entirely cool and self-possessed, which could hardly be said of the young naval officer.

By this time Mr. Alwayn had opened the front door of the office, and gone in. The detective backed in after him, and then pushed Christy in after the consul. The ruffians saw that they were losing their game, and they rushed upon the door. One of them crowded his way in, but M. Rubempré, in a very quiet way, delivered a blow on the end of the assailant's nose, which caused him to retreat, with the red fluid spurting from the injured member.

Taking his place, two others pushed forward, and aimed various blows at the two defenders of the position; but both of them were skilled in this sort of play, and warded off the strokes, delivering telling blows in the faces of the enemy. Mr. Alwayn had partially closed the door; but he was not so cowardly as to shut out his two volunteer defenders. As soon as they understood his object, they backed in at the door, dispersing the ruffians with well-directed blows, and the consul closed and locked the door. Before any further mischief could be done, the police came and dispersed the rioters. The consul fared better on this occasion than on several others, in one of which he was quite seriously injured.

As soon as order was restored, Mr. Alwayn conducted his defenders to his office, where he thanked them heartily for the service they had rendered him. During the *mêlée* M. Rubempré had tried to address the ruffians in broken French, for he did not for a moment forget his assumed character. He used the same "pigeon-talk" to the consul, and Christy, in the little he said, adopted the same dialect.

"He planted a heavy blow with his fist under the ear of his assailant."

"I see you are not Americans, my friends, " said the official.

"No, saire; we are some Frenchmen, " replied the detective, spreading out his two hands in a French gesture, and bowing very politely.

"Being Frenchmen, I am not a little surprised that you should have undertaken to defend me from this assault, " added Mr. Alwayn.

"Ze Frenchman like, wat was this you call him, ze fair play; and ve could not prevent to put some fingers in tose pies. Ver glad you was not have the head broke, " replied M. Rubempré, with another native flourish. "*Mais*, wat for de *canaille* make ze war on you, saire? You was certainment un gentleman ver respectable. "

Mr. Alwayn explained why he had incurred the hostility of the blockade-runners and their adherents, for he was sometimes compelled to protest against what he regarded as breaches of neutrality, and was obliged in the discharge of his duty to look after these people very closely, so that he was regarded as a spy.

"Oh! it was ze blockheads, was it? " exclaimed the Frenchman.

"Hardly the blockheads, " replied the consul, laughing at the blunder of the foreigner. "It is the blockade-runners that make the trouble. "

"Blockade-runners! *Merci.* Was there much blockadeers here in ze islands? " asked M. Rubempré, as though he was in total ignorance of the entire business of breaking the blockade.

"Thousands of them come here, for this is about the nearest neutral port to Wilmington, where many of this sort of craft run in. "

"Wilmington was in Delaware, where I have seen him on ze map. "

"No, sir; this Wilmington is in North Carolina. If you look out on the waters of the harbor, half the vessels you see there are blockade-runners, " added the consul. "And there are more of them at St. George's. It was only yesterday that a steamer I believe to be intended for a man-of-war for the Confederacy came into the port of St. George's, and I have been much occupied with her affairs, which is probably the reason for this attempt to assault me. "

"Ze *man*-of-war, " repeated the Frenchman. "Ze war, *c'est la guerre; mais* wat was ze man? "

"She is a vessel used for war purposes. "

"*She!* She is a woman; and I think that steamer was a woman-of-war. "

The consul laughed heartily, but insisted upon the feminine designation of the steamer.

"What you call ze name of ze man-of-war? " asked M. Rubempré, putting on a very puzzled expression of countenance.

"The Dornoch, " replied Mr. Alwayn.

"The D'Ornoch, " added the detective. "How you write him—like zis? " and he wrote it on a piece of paper by his own method.

"Not exactly, " replied the consul, writing it as given in English.

"How long ze Dornoch will she stop in zat port? " asked the Frenchman, in a very indifferent tone, as though the answer was not of the least consequence to him.

"Not long; I heard it stated in St. George's that she would get her supplies and cargo on board to-day and to-morrow, and will sail before dark to-morrow night, " replied Mr. Alwayn. "The government here ought not to allow her to remain even as long as that, for she is plainly intended for a Confederate cruiser, and my men inform me that she has six great guns, and fifty men. "

M. Rubempré obtained all the information the consul was able to give him, and much of it was of great importance. The official was under obligations to the two strangers, and he seemed not to suspect that either of them was an American, much less a naval officer. They took their leave of him in the politest manner possible, and were shown to the door by the consul.

"I am not quite sure that all his information is correct, and we must investigate for ourselves, " said the detective when they were in the street. "But this affray is bad for us, and I was very sorry when you interfered, Christophe. "

"You did not expect to see me fold my arms when a representative of the United States, and under our flag, was attacked by a lot of ruffians? " demanded Christy, rather warmly, though he spoke in French.

"I know you could not help it, and I did my best to aid you, " added M. Rubempré. "I only mean that it was unfortunate for us, for when we go about on the islands, we may be recognized by some of that mob. We must go back to the hotel. "

In a few minutes more they were at the Atlantic, where the Frenchman, with his usual flourish, ordered a carriage to be ready in half an hour, adding that he was about to dress for some visits he was to make in St. George's. They went to their rooms, and each of them changed his dress, coming out in black suits. The master wore a frock coat, but the servant was dressed in a "claw-hammer, " and looked like a first-class waiter.

It is about a two hours' ride over to St. George's, and Christy enjoyed the excursion as much as though there had not been a blockade-runner in the world. The town, with even its principal street not more than ten feet wide, reminded him of some of the quaint old cities of Europe he had visited with his father a few years before. But M. Rubempré was bent on business, and the delightful scenery was an old story to him. They took a boat at a pier, and for an hour a negro pulled them about the harbor. There were quite a number of steamers in the port, long, low, and rakish craft, built expressly for speed, and some of them must have been knocked to pieces by the blockaders before the lapse of many weeks, though a considerable proportion of them succeeded in delivering their cargoes at Wilmington or other places.

The visitors looked them over with the greatest interest. They even went on board of a couple of them, the detective pretending that he was looking for a passage to some port in the South from which he could reach Mobile, where his brother was in the Confederate army. No one could doubt that he was a Frenchman, and on one of them the captain spoke French, though very badly. M. Rubempré's good clothes secured the respect and confidence of those he encountered, and most of the officers freely told him where they were bound, and talked with great gusto of the business in which they were engaged. But none of them could guarantee him a safe passage to any port on the blockaded coast.

The excursion in the boat was continued, for the visitors had not yet seen the steamer they were the most anxious to examine. The detective would not inquire about this steamer, fearful that it might be reported by the negro at the oars, and excite suspicion. But at last, near the entrance to the harbor, the boatman pointed out the Dornoch, and told them all he knew about her. There were several lighters alongside, discharging coal and other cargo into her.

M. Rubempré, in his broken English, asked permission to go on deck, and it was promptly accorded to him. He was very polite to the officers, and they treated him with proper consideration. There were no guns in sight, and the steamer looked like a merchantman; but if she had been searched, her armament would have been found in the hold. The visitor again repeated his desire to obtain a passage to the South; and this request seemed to satisfy the first officer with whom he talked. He was informed that the steamer would sail about five on the afternoon of the next day, and he must be on board at that time, if he wished to go in the vessel. He learned many particulars in regard to her.

CHAPTER XI

AN UNEXPECTED RENCONTRE

It was lunch-time when the visitors landed, and they proceeded to the St. George's Hotel in Market Square, to attend to this mid-day duty. In the coffee-room they found quite a number of guests, and the only spare seat the detective found was at a large table at which a gentleman in uniform was seated.

"Wit your permis-si-on, I take one of the places here, " said M. Rubempré with his politest flourish.

"Certainly, " replied the gentleman, as politely as the Frenchman; and he seated himself at the table, Christy remaining standing.

"*Demandez un garcon*" (ask for a waiter), "Christophe. " Then in French he asked the stranger opposite him if he spoke that language.

"A little, sir; but I am not fluent in it, " replied the gentleman in the same language.

"Ah, my dear sir, you speak very well; and you have the Parisian accent, " added the Frenchman, who, like his countrymen, counted upon the effect of a little well-administered flattery.

"You are very kind to say so, sir. I have been in Paris a few months, and was always able to make my way with the language, " said the stranger, evidently pleased with the commendation bestowed upon his French accent; for many people take more pride in their foreign accent than in the proper use of their own language.

"Christophe, find a place for yourself, and order what you desire, " continued the Frenchman, as a waiter, summoned by the acting servant, presented himself to take the order.

At this moment a gentleman behind the detective vacated his place at the table, and Christy took a seat close to his companion. The lunch of both was ordered, and the stranger opposite had but just commenced his meal. M. Rubempré "laid himself out" to make himself as agreeable as possible, and he seemed to be succeeding admirably, for the stranger appeared to be absolutely charmed with him. Speaking slowly and clearly, so that the person in uniform, who did not speak French fluently, could understand him, he told him all about his brother in the Confederate army, and strongly expressed his desire to join him, and perhaps the army, for he had very strong sympathy for the right in the great conflict; in fact, he was disposed to engage in fighting for the right.

Then he inquired of his new friend what wine was the best in the island. The stranger preferred sherry, but perhaps a Frenchman might take a different view of the subject. M. Rubempré ordered both sherry and claret, and then filled the glasses of his *vis-a-vis* and his own. He did not offer any to his servant, for he knew that he never touched it. They drank claret first to each other's health.

"You are in the military, my friend? " continued the detective.

"No, sir; I am a sailor. Allow me to introduce myself as Captain Rombold, of the steamer Dornoch. "

"I am extremely happy to make your acquaintance, Captain Rombold. To reciprocate, I am M. Rubempré, of Paris, " added the Frenchman, as he filled his companion's glass, and they tippled again with an abundance of compliments. "I presume that you are in the British navy, Captain Rombold? "

"At present I am not, though I was formerly in that service, and resigned to engage in a more lucrative occupation. "

"Indeed, what could be better than the position of an officer in the Royal navy? "

"I am now a commander in the navy of the Confederate States, " added the captain, looking with interest into the face of his companion. "I am taking in coal and cargo, and shall sail at five to-morrow afternoon for Wilmington. "

"Is it possible? " said M. Rubempré, who appeared to be greatly impressed by what was said to him. "I wish I was a sailor, but I am not. You will break through the blockade? "

"I apprehend no difficulty in doing that, for the Dornoch is good for fourteen knots an hour, and most of the Federal fleet cannot make more than twelve. "

Christy was very glad to hear this acknowledgment of the speed of the intended cruiser, for it assured him that the Chateaugay could outsail her. The two gentlemen at the other table passed the wine very freely, and both of them seemed to be considerably exhilarated; but he was glad to perceive that his friend allowed the captain to do the most of the talking. The lunch was finished at last, and both of them rose from the table.

"I am exceedingly obliged to you, M. Rubempré, for the pleasure I have derived from this interview, " said Captain Rombold, as he grasped the hand of his companion. "I have had more practice with my French than for several years, and I take great delight in speaking the language. I hope we shall meet again. "

"Thanks! Thanks! I am very sure that we shall meet again; and almost as sure that we shall meet fighting for the right, " added the Frenchman.

"But I hope you will be a passenger on board of the Dornoch, as you suggested to me a little while ago. I will give you a good stateroom, though I cannot absolutely promise to take you to the port of our destination, for accidents may happen in the midst of the blockaders."

"If I can go with you, my dear Captain Rombold, I shall be on board of your ship by four to-morrow afternoon, " replied the detective, as he took the hand of his new friend for the last time.

Christy had finished his lunch, and they left the hotel together. The carriage in which they had come called for them at the appointed time, and they returned to Hamilton. The conversation was continued in French, so that the driver was none the wiser for what he heard. At the Atlantic they went to their rooms, where the information they had obtained was collaborated, and written down in French, the detective concealing it in a belt pocket he wore on his body.

"The wonder to me has been that these officers talked so freely, " said Christy, as they seated themselves at a window. "They talked to you as plainly as though you had been their friend for life. "

"Why shouldn't they? They can't help knowing that I am a Frenchman; and I am sorry to say that my countrymen, like so many of the English, sympathize with the South in the great Civil War. They take me for a friend at once. Besides, as they understand the matter here, why should these blockade-runners, or even the Confederate commander, object to telling what they are going to do. There will be no mail steamer to New York till after they have all gone off; and there is no telegraph yet. "

"Perhaps you are right, M. Rubempré; but I think a good deal more discretion would become them better, as they are likely to ascertain very soon, " added Christy.

"I suppose none of these people here would consider it possible or practicable to land at these islands and pick up the news, as we have done. This was my plan for Nassau, but I did not think of applying it to the Bermudas, till Captain Chantor told me his difficulty as to waiting for the Dornoch. "

"It seems to me we have done all we can do here, and there is nothing more to do. "

"That is very true; but I supposed it would take at least two days to do our business. We have been much more successful than I anticipated, and performed the duty in half the time I supposed it would require. But it was better to have too much time than too little. "

"It is nearly night now, and we have another day to spend here. "

"We can rest from our labors in the hope that our works will follow us. I am ready to do a good deal of sleeping in the time that remains to us, for we may not be able to sleep any to-morrow night, " added the detective as he threw himself on his bed, and was soon fast asleep.

Christy had slept enough the night before and during the morning; and he went out to take a walk in the town. He had taken off his suit of black, and put on the costume he had worn from the ship. He was inclined to see what there was in the town; and he walked about till it was dark, at which time he found himself in the vicinity of the Hamilton Hotel, the largest and best appointed in the town. He was dressed very plainly, but there was nothing shabby in his appearance; and he thought he would inspect the interior of the hotel.

He began to mount the piazza, when he suddenly halted, and started back with astonishment, and his hair almost stood on end. Directly in front of him, and not ten feet distant, sat his uncle, Homer Passford, of Glenfield, talking with a gentleman in uniform. The lantern that hung near him enabled him to see the features of the planter, but he could not see the face of the officer, with whom he was engaged in a very earnest conversation.

Christy's first impulse was to put a long distance between himself and his uncle, for his father's brother might identify him in spite of the color on his face. Such a discovery was likely to prove very annoying to him, and might render useless the information the detective and himself had obtained with so much trouble and risk. But the first question that came into his head was the inquiry as to what his uncle was doing in Bermuda. He was a Confederate of the most positive type, had done everything in his power for his government, as he understood it, and was willing to sacrifice his life and all that he had in the world in its service.

Colonel Passford must be there on some mission. He was a prominent and useful man in his State; and he would not have left it without some very strong motive. The nephew would have given a great deal, and exposed himself to no little peril, to be able to fathom this motive. He moved away from the piazza, and went upon it at another place. If he could hear some of the conversation he might be able to form some idea of the occasion of his uncle's visit.

Walking along the platform, he obtained a position behind Colonel Passford, and at the same time saw the face of the person with whom he was in conversation. He was not a little surprised to discover that the gentleman was Captain Rombold, commander of the Dornoch. He had hardly seen this officer, and he had no fear that he would recognize him; and, if he did, it was of little consequence, for he was there in the capacity of a servant. He took a vacant chair, turned his back to both of the speakers, and opened wide his ears. Probably nine-tenths of the people in the hotel were directly or indirectly concerned in the business of blockade-running; and secrecy was hardly necessary in that locality.

"As I say, Captain Rombold, we need more fast steamers, not to run the blockade, but to prey upon the enemy's commerce. In that way we can bring the people of the North to their senses, and put this unhallowed strife on the part of the Federals to an end, " said Colonel Passford.

"Well, Colonel, there are ships enough to be had on the other side of the Atlantic, and your money or your cotton will buy them, " added the naval officer.

"We have been rather unfortunate in running cotton out this last year. Several steamers and sailing vessels that I fitted out with cotton myself were captured by my own nephew, who was in command of a small steamer called the Bronx. "

"Of course those things could not be helped, " replied Captain Rombold; "but with the Gateshead and the Kilmarnock, larger and more powerful steamers than any that have been sent over, you can scour the ocean. They are ready for you when your money is ready. "

"It is ready now, for I have sacrificed my entire fortune for the purchase of these steamers; and I wait only for a vessel that will take me to Scotland, " replied Colonel Passford.

Christy promptly decided that the steamers mentioned should not be purchased to prey on the commerce of the United States, if he could possibly prevent it.

CHAPTER XII

AN IMPRACTICABLE SCHEME

Before the War of the Rebellion the commerce of the United States exceeded that of any other nation on the globe. The Confederate steamers, the Sumter, Alabama, Georgia, Florida, and other cruisers, swept our ships from the ocean, and the country has never regained its commercial prestige. Christy Passford listened with intense interest to the conversation between his uncle and the commander of the Dornoch, and he came to the conclusion that the latter was a naval officer of no ordinary ability. He evidently believed that the six-gun steamer in his charge was a command not worthy of his talent.

The Sumter, and some other vessels fitted out as privateers or war vessels, had already done a great deal of mischief to the shipping of the Northern States, and the young man fully realized the meaning of his uncle's intentions. Colonel Passford had been supplied with money by his government, with what he had raised himself, to purchase larger and more powerful steamers than had yet been obtained, and Captain Rombold appeared to be his confidant, with whom he must have been in communication for a considerable length of time.

Colonel Passford was going to England and Scotland to purchase the steamers mentioned and recommended as the kind required by his present companion. Christy could think of no manner in which he could serve his country so effectually as by preventing, or even delaying, the adding of these vessels to the navy of the South. But it was a tremendous undertaking for a young man. His uncle had certainly been very indiscreet in talking out loud about his plans; but it could hardly have been supposed that any loyal ears were near enough to hear them, for even the American consul was not safe in the islands.

Christy had doubled himself up in his chair, and pretended to be asleep, so that no notice was taken of him by the two gentlemen in conversation. He continued to listen till he heard a clock strike nine; but he obtained no further information, except in relation to the details of the colonel's plans. He was in great haste to get to England to purchase the vessels, and he had the drafts about him for the purpose. It was a vast sum, for the prices of desirable steamers had largely advanced under the demand for them for running the blockade.

"The easiest and quickest way for you to get to Liverpool or Glasgow is to go to New York, and there take a steamer to either of these ports, " suggested Captain Rombold.

"I dare not go to New York, for I should certainly be recognized there. My only brother is one of the most prominent agents of the Yankee government, and every passenger from Bermuda and Nassau is watched and dogged by detectives. It would not be prudent for me to go New York, for some pretext to rob me of the drafts I carry would be found, " replied Homer Passford.

"There may be a steamer from Bermuda in a week or a month, for there is no regular line, " added the naval officer.

"But there are regular lines from Havana, Mexico, Jamaica, and the Windward Islands, " suggested the agent of the Confederate government.

"Very true, and it is not necessary that I should make a port in the Confederate States before I begin my work on the ocean, " said Captain Rombold. "I have my commission from your government, with full powers to act, though I desired to make a port in the South, for, as you are aware, my wife is a native of Georgia, and is at her father's plantation at the present time. I captured two Yankee vessels off the Azores, and burned them. "

"I have no doubt about your powers; but can you not aid me in getting to England? " persisted the colonel.

"If you will take the chances, I can, Colonel Passford. If you will go on board of my ship to-morrow afternoon, and sail with me, I have no doubt we shall overhaul a steamer bound to England in the course of a week, for I will get into the track of these vessels. "

The agent promptly accepted this proposition, and soon after the conference ended, though not till the listener had taken himself out of the way, Christy had turned over in his mind a plan to terminate very suddenly his uncle's mission to purchase steamers, and to obtain possession of his drafts. M. Rubempré was adroit enough to accomplish almost anything, and he intended to have the detective make the colonel's acquaintance, and induce him to embark with them in the Eleuthera, pretending that he was going to France himself, and intended to intercept a French steamer from Progreso, whose course lay but a short distance south of the Bermudas.

But the plan suggested by Captain Rombold, and adopted by Colonel Passford, saved him from what the young officer regarded as his duty in the deception and capture of his uncle. When the Bellevite, while she was still the yacht of Captain Horatio Passford, had gone to the vicinity of Mobile, to the home of his father's brother, Homer had done all in his power to capture the steamer for the use of his government, and had made war upon her with armed vessels. He had done so conscientiously, believing it to be his duty to his country. This fact from the past made it easier for Christy to think of such a thing as the capture of his uncle, even in a neutral country.

The young man returned to the Atlantic Hotel. He found M. Rubempré still fast asleep, for his slumbers the night before had been very brief. He waked him, and told him all that had transpired during the evening, though not till the detective had ordered supper, which they had not partaken of so far. He stated the plan by which he had proposed to himself to prevent the purchase, for the present at least, of the Gateshead and Kilmarnock.

"Not a practicable plan, Christophe, " said the detective, shaking his head vigorously.

"Why not? " demanded Christy; and he explained the conduct of his uncle in regard to the Bellevite, when she was on a peaceful errand to convey her owner's daughter back to her home.

Then he related the attempt of the colonel's son, his cousin Corny, to capture the Bronx by a piece of wild strategy.

"But I do not object to your scheme on moral grounds, " interposed M. Rubempré. "Have you forgotten the affair of the Trent, when Messrs. Mason and Slidell were taken out of an English steamer? The British government made a tremendous tempest, and would certainly have declared war if the two envoys had not been returned to a British ship-of-war. The English flag waves over these islands, and they are supposed to be neutral ground. "

Fighting for the Right

"Neutral with a vengeance!" exclaimed Christy.

"If Colonel Passford had been carried off in the manner you thought of, the United States government would have been compelled to return him to these islands, with all his drafts and other property. I am very glad you found it unnecessary to carry out such a plot," said the detective, as a knock at the door announced that their supper was ready.

As Christy's plan was not in order, would be inutile, the business of the visitors at the islands was finished. Both of them slept till very late in the morning, and after breakfast lay down again and slept all the forenoon. The young man was afraid to go out of the hotel in the afternoon, fearful that he might meet his uncle. But his companion walked about the place, and visited the Hamilton, where he again encountered Captain Rombold, who introduced him to Colonel Passford; informing him that he was to be his fellow passenger. When the commander of the Dornoch told him that he might not make a Confederate port for some weeks, if at all, M. Rubempré decided not to take passage with him. Of course nothing was said that could be of any service to the detective, for he had already obtained the information he needed; but he assured himself that the steamer would sail at the time stated the day before.

Towards night the detective informed the landlord that he was to go to St. George's in the evening, paid his bill, and liberally rewarded the waiters. He had been over to the pier to look after the Eleuthera, and had found Joseph at his house. The boat was all right; her keeper had washed her out, and put everything in order on board of her. M. Rubempré returned to the hotel, and after supper Joseph came for the valises. It was quite dark when they left the place, and made their way to the pier. No one asked any questions, and the detective had caused it to be understood that he had engaged a boatman to take him to St. George's by water.

They went on board of the boat, and the fisherman assisted them in getting under way. The liberal skipper gave him another sovereign, adding that he need not say anything to any person about him and his servant. Joseph was profuse in his expressions of gratitude, for with so much money in his pocket he need not go a-fishing again for a month or more, and protested with all his might that he would not mention them to anybody.

The night was dark enough to conceal the Eleuthera after she got away from the shore, but not so dark that the skipper could not find his way around the reefs to Hogfish Cut. It was high tide, as it had been when they came inside of the rocks, and the boat went along quite briskly in the fresh west wind that was still blowing. Without accident or incident of importance, though the wind was ahead a portion of the way, the boat reached the Cut at about midnight. She stuck on a reef at this point, but very lightly, though it required half an hour or more to get her off. She made no water, and did not appear to be injured.

Without further mishap the Eleuthera passed through the opening in the reefs, and, taking the bearing of the light on Gibbs Hill, Mr. Gilfleur, as Christy began to call him from this time, laid his course to the south-west. The Chateaugay was not to show any lights, and there was nothing but the compass to depend upon; but a light was necessary to enable the skipper to see it. The lantern was used for this purpose, but it was carefully concealed in the stern.

"We are all right now, Mr. Passford; and you may turn in for about three hours, for I don't think we shall sight the ship in less than that time, " said the detective, as he put on his overcoat, for the night air was rather chilly, and his companion had already done so.

"I have no occasion to turn in, for I have slept enough at that hotel to last me for a week, " replied Christy. "It looks now as though we had made a good job of this visit to the Bermudas. "

"I think there can be no doubt of that, Mr. Passford; and there is an unpleasant surprise in store for your worthy uncle, " said Mr. Gilfleur, chuckling as he spoke.

"And perhaps for your accomplished friend Captain Rombold. We have both heard him say that he was regularly commissioned as a commander in the Confederate navy, and that his ship is armed with all proper authority to capture, burn, and destroy the mercantile marine of the United States. "

"But Captain Rombold is an ex-officer of the Royal navy, and you may depend upon it he will fight. There will be a naval battle somewhere in the vicinity of these islands to-morrow, and Captain Chantor will find that it will be no boy's play, " added Mr. Gilfleur.

"My father told me that he was a very able officer, and had already rendered good service, good enough to procure his rapid promotion. I liked the looks of his officers and crew, and I have no doubt they will give a good account of themselves."

"I hope so, for I am to be an American citizen: I have filed my first papers."

"I doubt not you will make a good and useful citizen; and your wonderful skill as a detective will make you very serviceable to your new country."

The conversation was continued for full three hours longer; at the end of which time they saw a dark body ahead on the port bow, and heard some rather gentle screams from a steam whistle.

CHAPTER XIII

AT THE END OF THE CHASE

Mr. Gilfleur estimated that the Eleuthera was at least fifteen miles from the light, and the whistles were not loud enough to be heard at that distance. Neither of the voyagers had any doubt that the dark mass ahead was the Chateaugay, and the skipper headed the boat for her. If it were not the ship that was expecting to pick up the visitors to the island, she would not be whistling in mid-ocean; and any other vessel would carry a head and side lights.

In half an hour more, for the Chateaugay appeared to have stopped her screw, the boat was within speaking distance, and the hail of Christy was answered. When she came alongside the steamer, the accommodation ladder was rigged out, several seamen came on board, and the voyagers hastened to the deck of the ship. Captain Chantor grasped the hand of the lieutenant, and then of the detective.

"I had some doubts whether or not I should ever see you again, " said the commander. "If they had discovered that one of you was a United States naval officer, they would have mobbed you. "

"As they did the American consul while we were there, " added Mr. Gilfleur.

"You will tell me of that later, " replied the captain, as he directed the officer of the watch to hoist in the boat and secure it as it had been before. "Now, come down into my cabin, and tell me your news, if you have seen something, even if you have not done anything, " he added.

"We were not expected to capture the islands, or make any demonstration; and we have been in only one fight, " replied Christy, to whom the commander turned as soon as they were seated at the table.

"Then you have been in a fight? " queried the captain.

"Only with the fists. We defended the United States consul when he was hard pressed, and we got him safely into his office by the time the police came upon the scene, " continued Christy. "But we have important information. Mr. Gilfleur will give it to you in full. "

"Pardon; but I very much prefer that Mr. Passford should be the historian of the expedition, " interposed the detective.

"But my friend and companion has been the principal actor; and I am sure I could not have done anything to obtain the information without him, " protested the lieutenant.

"Then it is all the more proper that you should tell the story, Mr. Passford, and spare Mr. Gilfleur's modesty, " said the captain.

It was agreed that Christy should be the narrator of the results of the expedition, and he first described the trip to Hamilton in the boat. Then he told about the assault on the consul, and in what manner they had defended him.

"I ought to inform you at once that the Dornoch was at St. George's harbor, and that she was to sail yesterday afternoon at five o'clock, " said Christy. "But she is bound to the southward, and her first mission is to intercept an English or French steamer, and put a Confederate commissioner, wishing to get to England, on board of her. This agent of the South happens to be my uncle. "

"The brother of Captain Passford? "

"Yes, Captain; and he is provided with funds to purchase two vessels—steamers, to be fitted up as men-of-war. "

"Then if he is your father's brother, you think, perhaps, that we ought not to molest him, " suggested the captain.

"Why, his graceless nephew even considered a scheme to entice him on board of our boat, under pretence of finding a passage to England for him, " interposed Mr. Gilfleur, laughing heartily at the suggestion of the commander.

"I believe in treating him like a Christian and a gentleman, for he is both of these; but I do not believe in letting him fill up the Confederate navy with foreign-built steamers, to ruin the commerce of my country, " replied the young officer with spirit. "My father would no more believe in it than I do. You should treat him, Captain Chantor, exactly as though he was nobody's brother or uncle. "

The commander clapped his hands as though he was of the same opinion as his passenger, and Christy proceeded with his narrative, describing their visit to the Dornoch and the blockade-runners at St. George's and Hamilton. The captain was very much amused at his interview in French with Captain Rombold, and his conversations with officers of other vessels they had boarded. The detective took his papers from the belt, and read the names of the steamers, and the ports for which they were bound.

"They were a very obliging lot of blockade-runners, " said the captain, laughing heartily at the freedom with which they had spoken.

"I don't suppose there is an American in the Bermudas at the present time besides Mr. Alwayn, the consul, " added the detective. "The blockade-runners have the islands all to themselves, or at least the two towns on them. They have plenty of money, and they spend it without stint or measure. They make business good, and the inhabitants take excellent care of them. It is no place for Americans; for everybody's sympathy is with the South. It seems to me that there is no danger of talking about their business anywhere in the islands. "

"They were speaking all the time to a Frenchman, who had considerable difficulty in using the English language, " said Christy. "All the talk with Captain Rombold was in French. "

The narrative was finished, and discussed at great length. The order had been given to the officer of the deck to go ahead at full speed, making the course south-east, after the Eleuthera had been hoisted on board and secured.

"It looks decidedly like a battle some time to-morrow, " said the commander thoughtfully.

"No doubt of it, " added Christy.

"If the Dornoch sailed at five o'clock yesterday afternoon, according to the arrangement, she must be over a hundred miles from the islands at this moment, " continued Captain Chantor thoughtfully, as he consulted his watch. "We can only conjecture his course, and that is the important thing for us to know. His first objective point is to intercept a steamer bound to England or France. If he runs directly to the southward he may miss the first one."

"If I were in his place I should run to the eastward, so as not to fall astern of any possible steamer bound to England," added Christy.

"That was the thought that first came to my mind," replied the commander, as he brought out a chart and spread it on the table. "For that reason I gave out the course to the south-east."

A careful examination of the chart and an extended calculation followed. It was agreed between the two naval officers that the Dornoch would go to the eastward till she fell into the track of vessels bound to the north-east from Jamaica, Cuban ports, or Mexico, and then put her head to the south-west. It was four o'clock in the morning, the cruiser had been out nine hours, and the captain dotted the chart where he believed she was at that moment.

"She has made all the easting necessary, and by this time she has laid her course about south-west," continued the commander. "Captain Rombold will not hurry his ship, for he has no occasion to do so, and he will naturally save his coal. If our calculations are correct, we shall see the Dornoch about noon to-day;" and he pointed to the conjunction of the two courses as he had drawn them on a diagram. "That is all; and we had better turn in."

A sharp lookout was maintained during the hours of the morning watch, for the conjectures and calculations of the captain might prove to be all wrong. It was possible that the Dornoch had proceeded directly to the southward, after making less easting than was anticipated. Nothing was seen of any steamer. But in the middle of the forenoon watch a long and rather faint streak of black was discovered in the east. The Dornoch was not exactly a blockade-runner, and doubtless she used soft coal, though anthracite was beginning to come into use in other than American steamers, for its smoke was less likely to betray them.

"I think we have figured this matter out correctly, Mr. Passford," said Captain Chantor, as they gazed at the attenuated streak of black.

"Captain Rombold is a very competent officer, and you and he seem to have agreed in your calculations, " added Christy.

The steamer to the eastward soon came in sight; she and the Chateaugay were headed for the same point, and by noon they were in plain sight of each other. In another hour they were within hailing distance.

"That is not the Dornoch, " said Christy decidedly.

"No; she is much larger than the Dornoch, " added Mr. Gilfleur.

"I am disappointed, " replied the captain.

The steamer showed the British flag, and went on her way to the south-west. The Chateaugay continued on her course without change till eight bells in the afternoon watch, when a heavier volume of smoke was descried in the north-east. No change was made in the course, and at the beginning of the second dog watch the craft from which the smoke issued could be seen with the naked eye. She was headed to the south-west, and it was evident that her course would carry her to the westward of the Chateaugay. The darkness soon settled down upon the ocean, and the port light of the stranger showed itself over the starboard quarter of the ship, proving that it crossed the wake of the other.

The action, if the steamer proved to be the Dornoch, must be deferred till the next morning. It was impossible to determine what she was in the darkness, and Captain Chantor ordered the course to be changed to correspond with that of the stranger, which manifested no disposition to get away from her. All night the two vessels maintained the same relative position, and both were making about ten knots an hour. At daylight in the morning the commander and Christy were on the quarter-deck, anxiously observing the stranger. She was carefully examined with the glasses.

"That is the Dornoch! " exclaimed Mr. Gilfleur, after a long inspection with the glass.

"No doubt of it, " added Christy.

"You are sure of it? " inquired the commander.

"We have both been on board of her, and I am perfectly sure of it," replied Christy, who proceeded to explain the details by which he identified her; and the captain was entirely satisfied.

The Dornoch was not more than two miles distant from the Chateaugay, for in the early morning hours the course had been changed a couple of points, to bring her nearer for examination. It was now a chase, and the chief engineer was instructed to give the ship her best speed. It was soon evident that the Dornoch was hurrying her pace, for her smoke-stacks were vomiting forth immense inky clouds.

"I doubt if Captain Rombold cares to fight with my uncle on board," said Christy. "He can see that the Chateaugay is of heavier metal than the Dornoch."

"I should suppose that it would be his first care, as perhaps he regards it as his first duty, to put his passenger on board of a steamer bound to England," added the commander. "It appears to be a question of speed just now."

The Chateaugay was driven to her utmost, and it was soon clear that she was too much for her antagonist. At two bells in the forenoon watch she was about a mile abreast of the chase, which had not yet shown her colors. The flag of the United States floated at the peak, and the commander ordered a shot to be fired across the forefoot of the Dornoch.

This was an order for her to come to; but, instead of doing so, she flung out the Confederate flag, and fired a shotted gun, the ball from which whizzed over the heads of the Chateaugay's officers on the quarter-deck.

CHAPTER XIV

AN EASY VICTORY

The shot from the Dornoch, which had evidently been intended to hit the Chateaugay, sufficiently indicated the purpose of her commander. On board of either steamer there could be no doubt in regard to the character of the other. Captain Chantor gave the order to beat to quarters, and in a few moments every officer and seaman was at his station.

Christy Passford went to his stateroom, buckled on his sword belt, and prepared his revolvers for use; for though he held no position on board of the Chateaugay, he did not intend to remain idle during the action, and was ready to serve as a volunteer. Mr. Gilfleur came to the open door of his room, and seemed to be somewhat astonished to observe his preparations.

"You appear to be ready for duty, Mr. Passford, though you are not attached to this ship, " said he.

"I have no position on board of the Chateaugay; but it would be quite impossible for me to remain inactive while my country needs my services, even as a supernumerary, " replied Christy.

"But what am I to do? " asked the detective, with a puzzled expression on his face.

"Nothing at all, Mr. Gilfleur; I regard you as a non-combatant, and I think you had better remain in your stateroom, " replied Christy. "But I must go on deck. "

The Frenchman followed him to the quarter-deck, and seemed to be inclined to take a hand in the conflict. He desired to be an American citizen, and possibly he believed he could win his title to this distinction in a battle better than by any other means. But he had no naval training, could be of no service at the guns, and was more likely to be in the way of others than to accomplish anything of value. It was a needless risk, and the captain suggested that his life was too valuable to his adopted country for him to expose himself before his mission had been accomplished. He stepped aside, but he was not willing to go below.

Fighting for the Right

"I desire to offer my services as a volunteer, Captain Chanter," said Christy, saluting the commander. "If you will assign me to any position on deck, though it be nothing more than a station at one of the guns, I will endeavor to do my duty."

"I have no doubt you would do your whole duty, Mr. Passford," replied the captain, taking him by the hand. "You can be of more service to me as an adviser than as a hand at a gun. It is plain enough that the commander of the Dornoch intends to fight as long as there is anything left of him or his ship. Your report of him gives me that assurance."

"I suppose by this time, Captain Chantor, you have arranged your plan for the action," added Christy, looking curiously into the face of the commander, though he had resolved to give no advice and to make no suggestions unless directly requested to do so.

"I suppose the only way is to pound the enemy till he has had enough of it, using such strategy as the occasion may require. According to your report we outweigh her in metal, and we have proved that we can outdo her in speed," replied Captain Chantor.

"But the Dornoch will have the privilege of pounding the Chateaugay at the same time," said Christy in a very low tone, so that no one could hear him.

"That is very true; of course we must expect to take as good as we send."

"But then what use shall you make of your advantage in speed and weight of metal?" asked the passenger very quietly. "We both believe that there is humanity in war as well as in peace."

At that moment a shot passed under the counter of the ship, and buried itself in the water a cable's length beyond her.

"That is good practice, Captain Chantor," said Christy. "That shot was aimed at your rudder; and I have no doubt Captain Rombold is seeking to cripple you by shooting it away."

"I believe in humanity in war; but I do not see where it comes in just now, except in a very general way," replied the captain.

"If the Dornoch cripples you, and then takes her own time to knock the Chateaugay to pieces, it will amount to the sacrifice of many lives," suggested the unattached officer.

"I should be very glad to have your opinion, Mr. Passford," added the commander.

"I certainly do not desire to thrust my opinion upon you, Captain Chantor; but as you have asked for it, I will express myself freely."

"Thank you, Mr. Passford."

"I should adopt the tactics of Commodore Dupont at Port Royal."

"In other words, you would keep sailing around the Dornoch."

"Precisely so. I would not give him a shot till I was out of the reach of his broadside guns."

"And then pound her with the midship gun. That is my idea exactly. Quartermaster, strike one bell."

"One bell, sir."

"Strike four bells, quartermaster," added the captain.

"Four bells, sir."

The Chateaugay was soon going ahead at her best speed, headed directly away from the Dornoch, and it would have looked to an observer as though she was running away from her. At any rate, the enemy made this interpretation of her movement, and immediately gave chase, opening fire upon the ship with her bow guns. Presently she fired her heavy midship gun, the shot from which would have made havoc if it had hit the mark. It was soon evident that the enemy's speed had been overrated, for the Chateaugay gained rapidly upon her. A shot from her heavy gun knocked off the upper works on one side of the Eleuthera, but did no other damage.

At the end of two hours even the heavy gun of the enemy could not carry its shot to the chase. It would have been easy enough to run away from the Dornoch; but this was by no means the intention of Captain Chantor. He was very cool and self-possessed, and he did not ask his passenger for any further suggestions. He understood his business thoroughly, though he had at first been disposed to make shorter work of the action than he had now adopted. As soon as he had obtained his distance, he gave the order to bring the ship about. Thus far he had not fired a gun, and the enemy had apparently had it all his own way.

The midship was in readiness to initiate the work of the Chateaugay. At the proper moment, the gunner himself sighted the piece, the lock string was operated, and the hull of the ship shook under the discharge. Christy had a spy-glass to his eye, levelled at the Dornoch. She had just begun to change her course to conform to that of the Chateaugay, and the observer on the quarter-deck discovered the splinters flying about her forecastle. The shot appeared to have struck at the heel of the bowsprit.

"That was well done, Captain Chantor, " said Christy.

"Excellently well done; but Mr. Turreton will improve when he gets his range a little better, " replied the captain.

At this moment the report of the Dornoch's great gun was heard again; but the shot fell considerably short of the Chateaugay. At the same time she was crowding on all the steam she could make, and Captain Chantor was manoeuvring his ship so as to maintain his distance. The midship gun was kept as busy as possible, and Mr. Turreton improved his practice very materially. Fought in this manner, the action was not very exciting. The ship followed her circular course, varying it only to maintain the distance. For several hours the unequal battle continued. The mainmast of the Dornoch had been shot away, and Christy, with his glass, saw several of the huge shots crash into her bow.

It was evident, after pounding her a good part of the day, that the enemy could not stand much more of this punishment. At eight bells in the afternoon watch she hauled down her flag. Christy had done nothing but watch the Dornoch, and report to Captain Chantor. As her flag came down, he discovered that her condition, after the last shot, was becoming desperate.

"She has settled considerably in the water, Captain Chantor, and that is evidently the reason why she hauled down her flag, " said Christy, just as the ship's company were cheering at the disappearance of the Confederate flag from the peak of the enemy.

"I was confident she could not endure much more such hulling as Mr. Turreton has been bestowing upon her, " replied the commander, after he had given the order to make the course directly towards the Dornoch.

Christy continued to watch the enemy's vessel. The ship's company were employed in stretching a sail over the bow, evidently for the purpose of stopping in whole or partially a dangerous leak in that part of the vessel; and she seemed to be in immediate peril of going to the bottom. They were also getting their boats ready, and the situation must have been critical. In a short time the Chateaugay was within hailing distance of her prize.

"Dornoch, ahoy! " shouted Captain Chantor, mounted on the port rail. "Do you surrender? "

"I do, " replied Captain Rombold; for Christy recognized his voice. "Our ship is sinking! "

By this time the havoc made by the big gun of the Chateaugay could be seen and estimated. The bow of the steamer had been nearly all shot away. Her bowsprit and her mainmast had gone by the board. Her bulwarks were stove in, and most of her boats appeared to have been knocked to pieces. In spite of the efforts to keep her afloat, it was plain that she was sinking; and Christy could see her settling in the water. The boats of the victor were promptly lowered, and crews sent away in them to the relief of the imperilled enemy. There were not more than sixty men on board of her, including the officers; and they were soon transferred to the deck of the Chateaugay.

Christy watched the boats with the most intense interest as they came alongside the ship; for he knew that his Uncle Homer was on board of the Dornoch, if the plans arranged at the hotel had been fully carried out. Captain Rombold came in the last boat, and Colonel Passford was with him. His nephew did not care to meet him just then. The Confederate commissioner came on deck; and Christy looked at him with interest from behind the mizzenmast. His expression testified to his grief and sorrow at the early failure of his mission. The young lieutenant could pity the man, while he rejoiced at his ill success in building up the navy of the Confederacy.

His attention was drawn off from his uncle by the sudden sinking of the Dornoch; and the vortex that followed her disappearance extended to the Chateaugay. Most of the officers and seamen had brought off the whole or a part of their clothing and other articles.

When Captain Rombold came on deck, Captain Chantor politely saluted him, and returned the sword he surrendered to him. Colonel Passford kept close to him; and Christy thought he looked dazed and vacant.

"While I must rejoice in my own good fortune, Captain Rombold, I can sympathize personally with a brave commander who has lost his ship, " said Captain Chantor, taking the hand of the late commander of the Dornoch.

"I thank you for your consideration, Captain. I am sorry to have been so easy a victim to your strategy; and I can reciprocate by congratulating you on your victory, though your better guns enabled you to knock my ship to pieces at your leisure, " replied Captain Rombold.

He then introduced Colonel Passford, and both of them were invited to the captain's cabin. The wounded were turned over to the surgeon, and the crew were sent below. It was clearly impossible for the ship to continue on her voyage with such an addition to her numbers; and the Chateaugay was at once headed back to New York.

CHAPTER XV

THE GENTLEMAN WITH A GRIZZLY BEARD

The addition of about sixty persons to the full complement of the ship's company of the Chateaugay made a considerable crowd on board of her; but accommodations were provided for all, and in three days the ship would deliver her human freight to the authorities in New York. The Dornoch had gone to the bottom with all her valuable cargo; but her captors would be remunerated in prize-money by the government, so that in a material point of view she was not lost to them, and there was one less cruiser to prey upon the commerce of the loyal nation.

Captain Rombold and Colonel Passford remained in the cabin all the rest of the day; but the next morning both of them went on deck to take the fresh air. Christy and Mr. Gilfleur were in the waist, and noticed them as soon as they appeared. They had had some conversation the evening before in regard to confronting the two most important prisoners, though without arriving at a conclusion.

"Of course I must meet my uncle, " said Christy. "I am not inclined to skulk and keep out of sight rather than meet him. Though I have assisted in doing him and his cause a great deal of mischief, I have done it in the service of my country; and I have no excuses to offer, and no apologies to make. "

"I was not thinking of excusing myself, or apologizing for what I have done, " replied the detective quite earnestly. "That is not the point I desire to make. Since I went to New York I have looked upon your country as my own; and I would do as much to serve her as I ever would have done for France. "

"What is your point, Mr. Gilfleur? " asked Christy.

"I do not object to your fraternizing with your uncle, Mr. Passford, if you are so disposed, " continued the Frenchman; "but the case is quite different with me. In the hotel at St. George's you were not presented to Captain Rombold, and you did not allow the Confederate commissioner to see and identify you. Neither of these gentlemen recognized you; but the captain of the Dornoch would certainly know me, for I talked with him a long time. "

"Suppose both of them know us: what difference will that make?" demanded the young lieutenant.

"It will explain to them in what manner we obtained our knowledge of the force and weight of metal of the Dornoch. While we had as good a right to be on shore in the Bermudas as the Confederates, if we were recognized our method of operations would be betrayed, and in my opinion that would be very bad policy, especially as we are to adopt the same strategy in the Bahamas."

"I see; and I agree with you, Mr. Gilfleur, that it will be good policy to keep our own counsel in regard to what we have done in the islands," added Christy, as he saw Captain Chantor approaching him.

"Good-morning, Mr. Passford. You and your uncle do not appear to be on very friendly terms, for I notice that you do not speak to each other."

"Our relations have always been friendly, even while I was in a rebel prison; but I have not happened to meet him since he came on board of the Chateaugay."

"I will present you to him as his nephew, if you desire me to do so," continued the commander with a smile.

"I thank you, Captain: I intended to speak to him when an opportunity came. But you will pardon me if I make a suggestion without being asked to do so," said Christy, speaking in a low tone; and he proceeded to state what had passed between him and Mr. Gilfleur. "I hope you have not mentioned the fact that Mr. Gilfleur and myself have been in the Bermudas."

"I have not, for it came to my mind that it would be very unwise to do so," replied the captain. "Besides, I was not at all inclined to tell Captain Rombold that I knew all about his ship, her size, the number of her ship's company, and the weight of his guns. A man does not feel just right when he finds he has been made the victim of a bit of strategy; and I was disposed to spare his feelings. He charges his misfortune altogether to his antiquated steamer, her failure in her promised speed, and the neglect of the Confederate commissioners to provide him with a suitable vessel."

"Mr. Gilfleur will keep out of the captain's sight during the run to New York; but I was acting as a servant when we met him, and did not sit at the same table. I will speak to my uncle now."

Captain Chantor attended him to the quarter-deck, where the commissioner was taking his morning walk. They fell in behind him as he was moving aft, so that he did not observe his nephew.

"Colonel Passford, I have a young gentleman on board of my ship who bears your name; allow me to present to you Lieutenant Christopher Passford, who is simply a passenger on the Chateaugay," said the captain, directing the attention of the commissioner to the young man.

"My nephew!" exclaimed Colonel Passford, as he recognized Christy, and extended his hand to him.

"I am very glad to see you, Uncle Homer, though I am sorry to meet you under present circumstances," replied the nephew, taking the offered hand. "I hope you are very well, sir."

"Not very well, Christy; and I am not likely to improve in health in a Yankee prison," answered the colonel with a very sickly smile.

"Probably my father will be able to obtain a parole for you, and he will be extremely glad to have you with him at Bonnydale," added Christy.

"The last time I met you, Christy, you looked upon me as a non-combatant, released me, and sent me on shore."

"I am not sure that I did wisely at that time."

"I was not taken in arms; and I could hardly be regarded as a prisoner of war."

"But you were engaged in the Confederate service, Uncle Homer, for you were shipping cotton for the benefit of the cause."

"But I was merely a passenger on board of the Dornoch."

"Yet you are a Confederate commissioner, seeking a passage in some vessel bound to England, for the purpose of purchasing steamers to serve in your navy, " added Christy with considerable energy, and without thinking that he was in danger of compromising himself and his companion in the visit to the Bermudas.

Colonel Passford stopped short, and gazed into the face of his nephew. He appeared to be utterly confounded by the statement, though he did not deny the truth of it.

"Without admitting the truth of what you say, Christy, I desire to ask upon what your statement is founded, " said the commissioner, after some hesitation.

"As you are on one side in this great conflict, and I am on the other, you must excuse me for not answering your question, " replied Christy very promptly, and declining to commit himself any farther.

"It is very sad to have our family divided so that we should be enemies, however friendly we may be personally, " added Colonel Passford in a tone that indicated his profound grief and sorrow.

"I know how useless it is for us to discuss the question, Uncle Homer, for I am sure you are as honest in your views as my father is in his. "

"I have no desire to argue the question; but I believe the North will come to its senses in good time—when the grass grows in the streets of New York, if not before. "

"You will have an opportunity to see for yourself, Uncle Homer, that New York was never so busy, never so prosperous, as at the present time; and the same may be truthfully said of all the cities of the North, " replied Christy with spirit.

"Sail, ho! " shouted the lookout forward.

An hour later the sail was reported to be a steamer, bound to the westward, and her streak of black smoke indicated that she was English. She was low in the water, had two smoke-stacks, and presented a very rakish appearance. She was a vessel of not more than eight hundred tons, and her build was quite peculiar. It was evident that she was a very fast steamer. But she seemed to have no suspicions in regard to the character of the Chateaugay.

Christy left his uncle, and went to the ward room, where he found Mr. Gilfleur in his stateroom. He desired the advice of the Frenchman before he said anything to the captain in regard to the approaching sail. Together they had looked over all the steamers in the harbor of St. George's, and those on board of them were not disposed to conceal the fact that they were to run the blockade as soon as they could get over to the coast of the United States.

"What have you been doing to yourself, Mr. Gilfleur? " asked Christy, as soon as he discovered the detective, for he had completely changed his appearance, and looked like an elderly gentleman of fifty, with a full beard, grizzled with the snows of many winters.

"I don't care to be shut up in this stateroom during the voyage to New York, " replied the Frenchman with a pleasant laugh. "This is one of my useful costumes, and I don't believe Captain Rombold will recognize me now. "

"I am very sure he will not, " added Christy, looking him over, and wondering at the skill which could so completely change his appearance.

"I want you to see the steamer which is approaching, bound to the westward. If I am not mistaken, we have seen her before. "

"I am all ready, and I will go on deck with you; but you must contrive to let the captain know who I am, or he will order me below, or have too much to say about me, " replied the detective, as he followed Christy to the quarter-deck.

Colonel Passford and Captain Rombold had seated themselves abaft the mizzenmast, and seemed to be interested in the reports respecting the approaching steamer. Christy called Captain Chantor to the rail, and explained what the commander had already scented as a mystery in regard to the gentleman with the grizzled beard. He laughed heartily as he gazed at the apparent stranger, and declared that he thought he might be another Confederate commissioner, for he looked respectable and dignified enough to be one.

"I think that steamer is the Cadet, Captain Chantor; and I have brought Mr. Gilfleur on deck to take a look at her. "

The Frenchman had no doubt the steamer was the Cadet, for she was peculiar enough in her build to be identified among a thousand vessels of her class. For some time they discussed the character of the vessel, and minutely examined her build and rig. Neither of them had any doubt as to her identity, and the passenger reported the result of the conference to the commander, who immediately ordered the American flag to be displayed at the peak; and gave the command to beat to quarters.

"We are over six hundred miles from any Confederate port, Mr. Passford," said the captain. "I should not like to have one of my captures surrendered to her owners."

"Of course you have your law books in your cabin, Captain; but I have studied them so much that I can quote literally from one bearing on this case," continued Christy. "'The sailing for a blockaded port, knowing it to be blockaded, is, it seems, such an act as may charge the party with a breach of the blockade.' Besides the evidence of her course, and that of the nature of her cargo, there are two witnesses to the declaration of the captain that he was intending to run into Wilmington."

"She has come about, and is running away from you, Captain!" exclaimed the passenger, who was the first on the quarter-deck to notice this change.

The commander ordered a gun to be fired across her bow, for the Cadet was hardly more than a quarter of a mile from the Chateaugay. No notice was taken of the shot, and a moment later the midship gun sent a shot which carried away her pilot-house and disabled the wheel.

CHAPTER XVI

AMONG THE BAHAMAS

"I am sorry to disturb you, gentlemen, but I feel obliged to ask you to retire to my cabin until this affair is settled, " said Captain Chantor, addressing Colonel Passford and Captain Rombold.

"I beg your pardon, Captain Chantor, but do you consider that you have a right to capture that steamer? " asked the late commander of the Dornoch, who seemed to be very much disturbed at the proceedings of his captor.

"Undoubtedly; and I have no doubt I shall be able to procure her condemnation on the ground that she is loaded for a Confederate port, no other than Wilmington, and has the 'guilty intention' to run the blockade. "

"I don't see where you could have obtained the information that enables you to make sure of her condemnation at the very first sight of her, " replied the Confederate officer.

"Well, Captain Rombold, if I succeed in proving my position before the court, out of the mouth of Captain Vickers, her commander, would that satisfy you? " asked the commander with a cheerful smile. "But you must excuse me from discussing the matter to any greater length, for I have a duty to perform at the present time. "

The Chateaugay was going ahead at full speed when the two gentlemen retired from the quarter-deck. She stopped her screw within hail of the Cadet. Her crew were clearing away the wreck of the pilot-house; but the destruction of her steering gear forward did not permit her to keep under way, though hands were at work on the quarter-deck putting her extra wheel in order for use. Of course it was plain enough to the captain of the Cadet that the Chateaugay, after the mischief she had done with a single shot, could knock the steamer all to pieces in a few minutes.

The first cutter, in charge of Mr. Birdwing, the executive officer, was sent on board of the disabled steamer, and Christy was invited to take a place in the boat. Captain Vickers was a broken-hearted man when he realized that his vessel was actually captured by a United States man-of-war.

"Do you surrender, Captain Vickers? " said Mr. Birdwing, as he saluted the disconsolate commander.

"How did you know my name? " demanded he gruffly.

"That is of no consequence, Captain Vickers. You will oblige me by answering my question. Do you surrender? " continued the lieutenant.

"I don't know that I can help myself, for this steamer is not armed, and I can make no resistance, " replied the captain. "I had no idea that ship was a Yankee gunboat. "

"But we had an idea that this was a blockade-runner, " added Mr. Birdwing, as he proceeded to take formal possession of the vessel, and called for her papers.

An examination was made into the character of the cargo, which consisted largely of arms and ammunition. The extra wheel was soon in working order. Before noon a prize crew was put on board, and both vessels were headed for New York. In three days more the Chateaugay was at anchor off the Navy Yard, with the Cadet near her. The return of the ship caused a great deal of surprise, and one of the first persons to come on board of her was Captain Passford. He gave his son his usual warm welcome.

Christy gave his father the narrative of the brief voyage, and astounded him with the information that his brother was on board. The two brothers had not met since they parted at the plantation near Mobile, and the meeting was as tender as it was sad; but both of them refrained from saying anything unpleasant in regard to the war. The prisoners were taken from the Chateaugay by a tender, and conveyed to Fort Lafayette; but Captain Passford soon obtained a parole for his brother, which he consented to give for a limited period.

"I suppose the Chateaugay will sail again by to-morrow, Christy; but you will have time to go home and see your mother and sister. I am so busy that I cannot go, and you must take Uncle Homer with you," said his father.

They landed on the New York side, and took a carriage for the station. Perhaps the streets of the great city were never more crowded with all kinds of vehicles, and especially with wagons loaded with merchandise of all kinds. They passed up Broadway, and Colonel Passford was silent as he witnessed the marvellous activity of the city in the midst of a great war.

"I think you will not be able to find any grass growing in the streets of New York, Uncle Homer, " said Christy, as they passed the Park, where the crowd seemed to be greater than elsewhere.

"There is certainly no grass here, and I am surprised to see that the city is as busy as ever, " replied the commissioner in a subdued tone. "We have been told at the South that business was paralyzed in the cities of the North, except what little was created by the war. "

"The war makes a vast amount of business, Uncle Homer, " added Christy.

But the gentleman from the South was not disposed to talk, and he soon relapsed into silence. Mrs. Passford and Florry were very much astonished to see Christy again so soon, and even more so to meet Uncle Homer; but his welcome was cordial, and nothing was said about the exciting topic of the day. The visitor was treated like a friend, and not an enemy, and everything was done to make him forget that he was not in his own home.

Early the next morning the young lieutenant hastened to report on board of the Chateaugay, where Mr. Gilfleur had remained, though he had divested himself of his disguise as soon as Captain Rombold was conveyed to other quarters. They were kept very busy that day giving their depositions in regard to the character of the Cadet, and of the admissions of Captain Vickers in regard to his intention to run the blockade. The ship had been coaled, and the next day she sailed again. She gave the Bermudas a wide berth, for she had another mission now, though she could probably have picked up one or two more of the blockade-runners Christy and his companion had seen in the harbor of St. George's.

Four days from Sandy Hook, very early in the morning, Abaco light was seen; and about fifty miles south of it was Nassau, on the island of New Providence, a favorite resort for blockade-runners at that time. The mission of the detective was at this port. Christy had again volunteered to be his companion, and they desired to get into the place as they had done in the Bermudas, without attracting the attention of any one, and especially not of those engaged in loading or fitting out vessels for the ports of the South.

As soon as the light was discovered, Captain Chantor ordered the course of the ship to be changed to east; and till eight bells in the afternoon watch she continued to steam away from the Great Abaco Island. It was his intention to avoid being seen, though there was a chance to fall in with a blockade-runner. Standing to the south-west the last part of the day, the light at the Hole in the Wall, the southern point of Great Abaco Island, was made out in the evening. South-east of this point is the northern end of Eleuthera Island, where the Egg Island light could be seen. This was the locality where Mr. Gilfleur had decided to begin upon his mission.

His boat had been repaired by the carpenter after the shot from the Dornoch struck it, and it was now in as good condition as it had ever been. At eleven o'clock in the evening the Eleuthera was lowered into the water, with a supply of provisions and water, and such clothing and other articles as might be needed, on board. The weather was as favorable as it could be, with a good breeze from the north-west.

"Now, Mr. Gilfleur, I hope you will bring back as important information as you did from the Bermudas, " said the captain, when the adventurers were ready to go on board of the boat.

"I hope so myself; but I don't know, " replied the Frenchman. "I expect to find the Ovidio at Nassau; and, like the Dornoch, she is intended for a man-of-war. Mr. Passford and I will do the best we can. "

"How long do you mean to be absent on this business? "

"About three days, as well as I can judge, though I have not had a chance to look over the ground. I have no doubt there are blockade-runners there, and we shall ascertain what we can in regard to them."

"I shall expect to pick you up to the eastward of the Hole in the Wall, and on the fourth night from the present time, " added the captain. "You know that the navigation of this region is very dangerous. "

"I am aware of it; but I have been here before, and I provided myself with a good chart in New York. I have studied it very attentively, and I have the feeling that I can make my way without any difficulty, " replied Mr. Gilfleur confidently.

Christy had already taken his place in the boat, and the detective soon followed him. It seemed something like an old story, after his experience in the Bermudas. The Eleuthera was cast off, the captain wished them a safe and prosperous voyage to their destination. The mainsail had been set, and the breeze soon wafted the boat away from the ship. The Chateaugay started her screw, and headed off to the eastward again, on the lookout for blockade-runners.

"Here is a light ahead, " said Christy, after his companion had set the jib, and taken the helm.

"That is Egg Island light, about forty miles from Nassau. Our course is south-west, which gives us a fair wind, " replied the skipper. "Now, Mr. Passford, you can do as you did on our former voyage in the Eleuthera: turn in and sleep till morning. "

"That would not be fair. I will take my trick at the helm, as it seems to be plain sailing, and you can have your nap first, " suggested Christy.

"No; I slept all the afternoon in anticipation of to-night, and I could not sleep if I tried, " the skipper insisted. "By the way, Mr. Passford, I am somewhat afraid that the name of our boat may get us into trouble. "

"Why so? " asked the other curiously.

"The island on our port hand is Eleuthera, about forty miles long. Of course it is well known at Nassau, and it may cause people to ask us some hard questions. We may even stumble upon the boat's former owner, who would claim her. "

"We could buy her, or another like her, in that case, " suggested Christy. "The name is painted on the stern board, and we might remove it, if necessary. "

Mr. Gilfleur said so much about it that Christy finally turned in, and was soon fast asleep. He did not wake till daylight in the morning.

He found that the boat was headed towards an island, while in the distance he saw the light on Hog Island, with a portion of the town of Nassau, and a fort. The skipper had his chart spread out on the seat at his side, and he was watching it very closely.

"Good-morning, Mr. Gilfleur. I suppose that must be Nassau ahead of us."

"Yes; that is Nassau. I expected to get here earlier in the morning than this, and I am not a little afraid to sail into the harbor at seven o'clock in the morning, as it will be before we can get there. The wind died out in the middle of the night, though I got it again very early this morning. I must get to the town in some other way. The land on the port is Rose Island, and Douglas Channel is just this side of it. I am going through that, and shall make my way to the back side of the island, where we can conceal the boat."

"I should say that would be a good idea," added Christy, as he took in the plan. "The water is as clear as crystal here, and you can see the bottom as plainly as though nothing came between your eye and the rock."

The skipper stationed his companion on the bow of the boat to watch for rocks; but none interfered with the progress of the Eleuthera. She sailed to the back side of the island of New Providence, where they found a secluded nook, in which they moored the craft.

CHAPTER XVII

THE LANDING AT NEW PROVIDENCE

The water was so clear that the bottom could be seen at all times, the white coral rock greatly assisting the transparency. From Douglas Channel, through which the boat had passed, the chart indicated that it was twenty miles to the point where the skipper desired to land, and it was nearly eleven o'clock when the Eleuthera ran into the little bay, extending over a mile into the island, and nearly landlocked. The shore was covered with tropical vegetation, including cocoa-nut palms, loaded with fruit, with palmettoes, wild palms, and many plants of which Christy did not even know the names.

"We could not have anything better than this, " said Mr. Gilfleur, as he ran the boat into a tangle of mangroves and other plants.

"This bay appears to be about five miles from the town of Nassau, and I should say that no person is likely to see the boat if it should stay here for a month, " replied Christy, as he measured the distance across the island with the scale his companion had prepared.

"It will not take us long to walk that distance. There are all sorts of people in Nassau at the present time, as there were in St. George's and Hamilton; and we shall pass without exciting any particular attention. "

"I think we had better look out for a cleaner place to land than this, for the mud seems to be about knee-deep, " suggested Christy, as he tested the consistency of the shore with an oar.

"But there is hard ground within four feet of the water. I have a board in the bottom of the boat with which we can bridge the mud, " replied the skipper. "But I think we had better have our lunch before we walk five miles. "

"I am in condition to lunch, " added Christy.

The sails had been furled, and everything put in order on board of the boat. The basket containing the provisions was brought out of the cuddy, and seated in the stern sheets they did ample justice to the meal. The detective had put on his suit of blue, and his

Fighting for the Right

companion dressed himself as he had done in Bermuda, though he was not to act the part of a servant on this occasion.

"It will not do to acknowledge that we are Americans, and it would not be prudent to claim that we are Englishmen, " said Mr. Gilfleur.

"Why not? We speak English; and you can pronounce it as well as I can, " argued Christy.

"Because we may be catechised; though I know London almost as well as I do Paris, I am afraid you might be caught. "

"I have been in London twice, though I don't know enough about it to answer all the questions that may be put to me, " added Christy.

"In that case we had better be Frenchmen, as we were before. We are not likely to find many people here who speak French, for the visiting portion of the population must be people who are engaged in blockade-running. Probably there are some Southern magnates here, attending to the business of the Confederacy. "

"They were here two years ago, when I was in Nassau for a few hours, on the lookout for steamers for their navy. I remember Colonel Richard Pierson, who was extremely anxious to purchase the Bellevite, which anchored outside the light, for there was not water enough to allow her to cross the bar, " said Christy, recalling some of the events of his first voyage in the steamer his father had presented to the government.

"Perhaps he is still in Nassau, " suggested Mr. Gilfleur, with a shade of anxiety on his face.

"He would not recognize me now, for I have grown a good deal, and I hardly saw him. He employed his son, a young fellow of eighteen, to act for him in obtaining information in regard to the Bellevite. The son's name was Percy Pierson, and when he tried to pump me in regard to the Bellevite, I chaffed him till he lost all patience. Then he proposed to put the owner of our steamer, for she had not then been transferred to the government, in the way of making a fortune. I told him that the owner was determined to get rid of the ship, though I only meant to say that he intended to pass her over to the government. At any rate, Percy believed she was for sale, and he smuggled himself on board of her. He was not discovered till we were under way; and we had to take him with us."

"What became of this Percy Pierson?" asked the detective.

"We brought him off with us when we fought our way out of Mobile Bay. Off Carisfort Reef light we put him on board of a schooner belonging to Nassau; and that was the last I know about him."

"But I hope he is not in Nassau now," said Mr. Gilfleur.

"I don't believe he is, for his brother was doing his best to get him into the Confederate army."

"You must keep your eyes wide open for this fellow, Mr. Passford," added the skipper earnestly. "If he should recognize you, our enterprise would be ruined."

"I don't believe there is the least danger of that, for I am a different-looking fellow from what I was two years ago. But I will look out sharply for him, and for his father."

"We had better speak nothing but French between ourselves, and break up our English when we are obliged to use it," Mr. Gilfleur concluded, as he returned the basket of provisions to the cuddy, and locked the door.

The board was put down on the mud, and they walked ashore, dry-shod. The temporary bridge was taken up, and concealed in a mass of mangroves. The Eleuthera was so well covered up with trees and bushes that she was not likely to be discovered, unless some wanderer penetrated the thicket that surrounded her. A gentle elevation was directly before them, so that they could not see the town.

"We must not walk ten miles in making five," said the detective, as he produced a pocket compass. "Our course, as I took it from the chart, is due north, though it may bring us in at the western end of the town."

"Then we can bear a little to the east, though if we get to the town it will not make much difference where we strike it," added Christy.

The land showed the remains of plantations which had flourished there in the palmy days of the island. The ruins of several mansions and many small huts were seen. Cocoa-nut palms and orange-trees were abundant. After they had walked about a mile, they came upon what had been a road in former days, and was evidently used to some extent still. Taking this road, they followed it till they were satisfied that it would take them to Nassau.

The appearance of the island soon began to improve. The trees showed that some care had been bestowed upon them, and an occasional mansion was noticed. Then the street began to be flanked with small houses, hardly better than huts, which were inhabited by the blacks. All the people they met were negroes, and they were as polite as though they had been brought up in Paris, for every one of the men either touched his hat or took it off to the strangers. The women bowed also; and both of the travellers returned the salutes in every instance.

As they proceeded, the houses became better, and many of them were used in part as shops, in which a variety of articles, including beer, was sold. Christy had seen the negroes of the Southern States, and he thought the Nassau colored people presented a much better appearance. At one of these little shops a carriage of the victoria pattern was standing. Doubtless the driver had gone in to refresh himself after a long course, for the vehicle was headed towards the town.

"I think we had better ride the rest of the way, if this carriage is not engaged, " said M. Rubempré, for they had agreed to use the names they had adopted in the Bermudas. "What do you say, Christophe? "

"I like the idea; I am beginning to be a little tired, for I have not walked much lately, " replied Christy.

At this moment the driver, a negro wearing a straw hat with a very broad brim, came out of the shop, wiping his mouth with the sleeve of his coat. He bowed with even more deference than the generality of the people. The strangers were not elegantly or genteelly dressed, but they wore good clothes, and would have passed for masters of vessels, so far as their costumes were concerned.

"Is this your carriage? " demanded M. Rubempré.

"Yes, sir," replied the man in good English.

"How far you must go to get into Nassau?" inquired the detective, mangling his English enough to suit the occasion.

"Two miles, sir."

"How much you make pay to go to Nassau in ze carriage?"

"Fifty cents."

"Feefty cents; how much money was zat?"

"Arn't you Americans?"

"*Non!*" replied M. Rubempré with energy. "We have come from ze France; but I was been in London, and I comprehend ze money of Eengland."

"Two shillings then," replied the driver, laughing.

"We go wiz you to ze Nassau," added the Frenchman, seating himself in the carriage, his companion taking a place at his side.

"Where do you want to go, sir?" asked the negro, as he closed the door of the victoria.

"We must go to Nassau," replied the detective, mangling his pronunciation even more than his grammar.

"Yes, I know; but where in Nassau do you wish to go? Shall I drive you to a hotel? The Royal Victoria is the best in the place."

"You shall take us to zat hotel."

For the sake of appearances, rather than for any other reason, each of the visitors to Nassau had brought with him a small hand-bag, containing such articles as might be useful to them. Having these evidences that they were travellers, it would be prudent to go to a hotel, though the want of more luggage had made the landlord in Hamilton suspicious of their ability to pay their bills.

Fighting for the Right

Christy found enough to do during the ride to observe the strange sights presented to his gaze, even in the outskirts of the town. The people were full of interest to him, and he wondered that his father had never made a winter trip in the West Indies in former years, instead of confining his visits to the more northern islands of the ocean.

The carriage arrived at the Royal Victoria Hotel, located on a ridge which has been dignified as a hill, a short distance in the rear of the business portion of the town. M. Rubempré produced his purse, which was well stuffed with sovereigns, more for the enlightenment of the clerk who came out when the vehicle stopped, than for the information of the driver, to whom he paid four florins, which was just double his fare.

"Do you speak French? " asked the guest in that language.

"No, sir; not a word of it, " though he understood the question.

"We must have two chambers for one, two, t'ree day. "

"All right; we have two that were vacated this morning, " replied the clerk, as he led the way to the office, where the Frenchman registered his name, and his residence as in Paris.

Christy wrote the name of Christophe Poireau, also from Paris. Then they chatted together in French for a moment, in order to impress the clerk and others who were standing near with the fact that they spoke the polite language. They were shown to two small chambers, well up in the air, for the hotel seemed to be as full as the clerk had suggested that it was. The blockade business made the town and the hotel very lively.

The newly arrived guests did not waste any time in their rooms, but entered at once upon the work of their mission. On the piazza they halted to size up the other visitors at the hotel. From this high point of view they could see the harbor, crowded with vessels.

CHAPTER XVIII

AN AFFRAY IN NASSAU

Christy's first care was to look about among the guests of the hotel gathered on the piazza, in order to ascertain if there was any person there whom he had ever met before. Very few of them were what could be classed as genteel people, and some of them were such people as one would not expect to see at a first-class hotel. They were dressed in seaman's garments for the most part, though not as common sailors; and doubtless many of them were commanders or officers of the vessels in the harbor.

Putting on an indifferent air he walked about the veranda, observing every person he encountered, as well as those who were seated in groups, engaged in rather noisy conversation, intermixed with a great deal of profanity. He breathed easier when he had made the circuit of the piazzas on the first floor, though there were two others on the stories above it, for he found no one he could identify as a person he had seen before.

There were quite a number of steamers in the harbor, or in that part of it which lies inside of the bar and in front of the town, with at least three times as many sailing craft. No doubt many of the latter, as well as the former, had brought cargoes of cotton from Confederate ports; for though the blockade was regarded as effective, and treated as such by foreign nations, many small vessels contrived to escape from obscure harbors on the Southern coast. Christy had been concerned in the capture of a considerable number of such. On the wharves were stacks of cotton which had been landed from these vessels, and several of them were engaged in transferring it to small steamers, for large ones were unable to cross the bar. But the visitors had no business with the vessels thus engaged, for they had completed their voyages, and were exempt from capture.

"I have taken not a few prisoners in or off Southern ports, and it would not greatly surprise me if I should meet some one I had met before, " said Christy, in French, as he resumed his seat by the side of the detective.

"Then I fear that your coming with me was a mistake, " replied M. Rubempré. "You must be extremely cautious, not only for your own protection, but because you may compromise me, and cause me to fail in the accomplishment of my mission here. "

"I should be sorry to interfere with your work, and I think we had better separate, " replied Christy, very much disturbed at the suggestion of his friend. "If I can do no good, I certainly do not wish to do any harm. "

"No, my friend; I cannot desert you, especially if you are in peril, " protested the detective. "How could I ever look your father in the face if I permitted you to get into trouble here? "

"I don't think I shall get into trouble, even if I am recognized by some person. This is not Confederate territory, though it looks very much like it; for all the people around us are talking secession, and the inhabitants sympathize with the South to the fullest extent. I could not be captured and sent to a Confederate State, or be subjected to any violence, for the authorities would not permit anything of the kind, " Christy argued with energy.

"I am not so sure of that. "

"I have no doubt in regard to my own safety; but if you appear to be connected with me in any manner, and I were identified as a United States naval officer, of course it would ruin your enterprise. For this reason I insist that we separate, and I will take a room at another hotel. "

Christy was determined, and in the end the detective had to yield in substance to him, though it was agreed, for reasons that seemed to be good, that M. Rubempré should change his hotel. They arranged to meet after dark in the grounds in the rear of the Royal Victoria, to consult in regard to the future.

"In the mean time I will do what I can to obtain information in regard to steamers bound to Confederate ports. I will still claim to be a Frenchman, and talk pigeon English, " continued Christy.

"If any misfortune happens to you, Christophe, I shall blame myself for it, " added the Frenchman.

"You cannot fairly do that, for it will not be through any fault of yours. If I fail to meet you as agreed, you can look for me. If you cannot find me, you must leave at the time agreed upon with Captain Chantor, whether I go with you or not. But I have no idea that anything will happen to prevent me from returning to the ship with you."

"His blood was boiling with indignation at the unprovoked assault."

"I could not leave without you," said the detective moodily.

"If you do not, you will be likely to get the Chateaugay into trouble; for if we did not return to her, she would probably come into this port after us."

"I will consider the matter before I assent to it," returned M. Rubempré, rising from his chair.

Christy was fully resolved not to endanger the mission of his companion, and he left the hotel. He walked slowly down Parliament to Bay Street, which is the principal business avenue of the town, running parallel to the shore. It was lined with shops, saloons, and small hotels on one side, and with the market and wharves on the other. He desired to see what he could of the place, and pick up all the information that would be serviceable to an officer of the navy.

As he passed a drinking-saloon a torrent of loud talk, spiced with oaths, flowed out from the place. Before he had fairly passed the door a violent hand was laid upon him, seizing him by the collar with no gentle grasp. The ruffian had fallen upon him from the rear, and he could not see who it was that assaulted him. The man attempted to drag him into the saloon; but he was evidently considerably affected by his potations in the place, and his legs were somewhat tangled up by the condition of his brain.

Christy attempted, by a vigorous movement, to shake off his assailant; but the fellow held on, and he found it impossible to detach his grasp. His blood was boiling with indignation at the unprovoked assault, and his two fists were clinched so tight that iron could hardly have been harder and tougher. He levelled a blow at the head of the ruffian, who still kept in his rear, and delivered it with all the power of his strong arm.

The assailant reeled, and released his hold, for his head must have whirled around like a top under the crashing blow it had sustained. Christy turned so that he could see the ruffian. He was a stalwart fellow, at least fifty pounds heavier than the young lieutenant. His nose was terribly disfigured, not by the blow of the young officer, for, twisted as it was, there was no sign of a fresh wound upon it. One glance was enough to satisfy Christy as to the identity of the ruffian.

Fighting for the Right

It was Captain Flanger, whose steamer Christy had captured, with a boat expedition sent out from the Bronx, in St. Andrew's Bay. He was a prisoner, but had escaped, and invaded the cabin of the Bronx, where he attempted to make Christy sign an order which would have resulted in delivering the steamer to the enemy. The heroic young commander, preferring death to dishonor, had refused to sign the order. The affair had culminated in a sort of duel in the cabin, in which Christy, aided by his faithful steward, had hit Flanger in the nose with his revolver.

The ruffian had sworn to be revenged at the time, and he seemed to have chosen the present occasion to wreak his vengeance upon the destroyer of his nasal member. The blow his victim had struck was a set-back to him; but he presently recovered the balance of his head which the shock had upset. It was plain enough that he had not given up the battle, for he had drawn back with the evident intention of using his clinched fists upon his adversary.

"Hit him again, Flanger! " shouted one of the brutal occupants of the saloon, who now filled the doorway.

The affair was rapidly becoming serious, and Christy was debating with himself whether or not he should draw a revolver he carried in his pocket; but he was cool enough to realize that he was on neutral ground, and that it would be very imprudent to be the first to resort to deadly weapons. He could not run away, for his self-respect would not permit him to do so. He braced himself up to meet the onslaught of the ruffian.

Flanger charged upon him, and attempted to plant a blow with his fist in the face of his intended victim; but the young officer parried it, and was about to follow up the movement with a blow, when Monsieur Rubempré rushed in between them, struck the assailant such a blow that he went over backwards. In fact, the man was too much intoxicated to stand without considerable difficulty.

At this moment a couple of colored policemen rushed in between the combatants. The tipplers in the saloon picked up their comrade, and stood him on his feet. The Nassau officers doubtless had a great deal of this sort of quarrelling, for drinking strong liquors was the principal occupation of the officers and crews of the blockade-runners while in port and on shore.

Fighting for the Right

"What is all this about? Who began this quarrel? " demanded one of them, as he looked from one party to the other in the battle.

"I was passing the door of this saloon, and did not even look into it, when that man rushed upon me, and seized me by the collar, " replied Christy. "I tried to shake him off, but I could not, and then I struck him in the side of the head. "

"Look here, you nigger! " shouted Captain Flanger. "It's none of your business who began it. "

"I shall arrest you for a breach of the peace, " said the policeman.

"I don't reckon you will. Do you see my nose? Look at it! Don't you see that it is knocked into a cocked hat? " said Flanger fiercely.

"I see it is; but what has that to do with this matter? " asked the negro officer.

"That man shot my nose off! " roared Flanger. "I am going to kill him for it, if it costs me my head! "

"You shall not kill him here, " protested the guardian of the peace. "You have been drinking too much, sir, and you must go with me and get sobered off. "

The two policemen walked up to him with the intention of arresting him; but he showed fight. He was too tipsy to make an effectual resistance. His companions in the saloon huddled around him, and endeavored to compel the policemen to let go their hold of him; but they held on to their prisoner till two more officers came, and Flanger was dragged out into the street, and then marched to the jail.

Christy was very much surprised that nothing was said to him by the officers about the affair in which he had been one of the principal actors. He had expected to be summoned as a witness against the prisoner they had taken, but not a word was said to him. He looked about to see if the detective was in sight, but he had disappeared.

"That was an ugly-looking man, " said a gentleman in the street, after the carousers had returned to the saloon. "I hope he has not injured you. "

"Not at all, sir; he was too drunk to do all he could have done if he had been in full possession of his faculties, for he is a much heavier person than I am, " replied Christy. "Why was I not summoned as a witness at his examination? "

"Oh, bless you, sir! they will not examine or try him; they will sober him off, and then discharge him. He is the captain of that little steamer near the public wharf. She is called the Snapper, and will sail for the States on the high tide at five o'clock. "

"Do you know to what port she is bound? " asked Christy.

"Mobile. "

The young officer walked down to the public wharf to see the Snapper.

CHAPTER XIX

AN OLD ACQUAINTANCE

The Snapper was quite a small craft, and looked like an old vessel; for she was a side-wheeler, though she had evidently been built for a sea-going craft. Whether Flanger had escaped from the Bellevite after being transferred to her from the Bronx, or had been regularly exchanged as a prisoner of war, Christy had no means of knowing. It made little difference; he was in Nassau, and he was thirsting for revenge against him.

The young officer did not feel that the brutal wretch had any reasonable cause to complain of him, and especially no right to revenge himself for an injury received while his assailant was the aggressor. He had done his duty to his country. He had been compelled to act promptly; and he had not aimed his revolver particularly at the nose of his dangerous assailant. Flanger was engaged in a foolhardy enterprise; and the mutilation of his nasal member had resulted very naturally from his folly.

His enemy was probably a good sailor, and he was a bold ruffian. Christy had captured the steamer loaded with cotton, in which he was all ready to sail from St. Andrew's Bay; and doubtless this was his first reason for hating the young officer. But no soldier or sailor of character would ever think of such a thing as revenging himself for an injury received in the strife, especially if it was fairly inflicted. The business of war is to kill, wound, and capture, as well as for each side to injure the other in person and property to the extent of its ability.

"Want a boat, sir?" asked a negro, who saw that Christy was gazing at the Snapper, even while he was thinking about his quarrel with Captain Flanger.

"Where is your boat?" asked the officer.

"Right here, sir," replied the boatman, pointing to the steps at the landing-place. "The best sailboat in the harbor, sir."

"I want to sail about this bay for a couple of hours," added Christy, as he stopped on the upper step to examine the craft.

Fighting for the Right

It was built exactly like the Eleuthera, though not quite so large.

"I saw you looking at the steamer there," said the boatman, pointing to the vessel in which Christy was interested. "Do you wish to go on board of her, sir?"

"No; I desire only to sail about the harbor, and perhaps go outside the bar. Can you cross it in this boat?"

"Yes, sir; no trouble at all about crossing it in the Dinah. Take you over to Eleuthera, if you like."

"No; I only want to sail about the harbor, and look at the vessels in port," replied Christy.

While he was looking at the boat, he became conscious that a young man, who was standing on the capsill of the wharf, was looking at him very earnestly. He only glanced at him, but did not recognize him. He had taken the first step in the descent of the stairs, when this person put his hand upon his shoulder to attract his attention. Christy looked at him, and was sure that he had seen him before, though he failed to identify him.

"How are you, Christy?" said the stranger. "Don't you know me?"

"Your face has a familiar look to me, but I am unable to make you out at first sight," replied the young officer, more puzzled as he examined the features of the young man, who appeared to be about twenty years old.

"You and I both have grown a great deal in the last two years, since we first met on this very wharf; but I am Percy Pierson, and you and I were fellow-voyagers in the Bellevite."

"I think you have changed in that time more than I have, or I should have recognized you," answered Christy very coldly, for he was not at all pleased to be identified by any person.

"You are a good deal larger than when I saw you last time, but you look just the same. I am glad to see you, Christy, for you and I ran a big rig over in Mobile Bay," continued Percy, as he extended his hand to the other.

Christy realized that it would be useless as well as foolish to deny his identity to one who knew him so well. A moment's reflection assured him that he must make the best of the circumstances; but he wished with all his might that he had not come to Nassau. He was particularly glad that he had insisted upon separating from Mr. Gilfleur, for the present encounter would have ruined his mission. The young man's father was Colonel Richard Pierson, a neighbor of Homer Passford; and he was a Confederate commissioner for the purchase of vessels for the rebel navy, for running the blockade. Doubtless the son was his father's assistant, as he had been at the time of Christy's first visit.

Percy was not a person of very heavy brain calibre, as his companion had learned from an association of several weeks with him. Christy believed that he might obtain some useful information from him; and he decided, since it was impossible to escape the interview, to make the best of it, and he accepted the offered hand. He did not consider the young Southerner as much of a rebel, for he had refused to shoulder a musket and fight for the cause.

"I begin to see your former looks, and particularly your expression, " said Christy. "I am very glad to see you, and I hope you have been very well since we met last. "

"Very well indeed. "

"Do you live here, Percy? "

"I have lived here most of the time since we parted on board of the Bellevite, and you put me on board of a schooner bound to Nassau. That was a very good turn you did me, for I believed you would take me to New York, and pitch me into a Yankee prison. I was very grateful to you, for I know it was your influence that saved me. "

This remark seemed to put a new face upon the meeting. Christy had done nothing to cause him to be set free; for the Bellevite, though she had beaten off several steamers that attempted to capture her, was not in the regular service at the time, her mission in the South being simply to bring home the daughter of her owner, who had passed the winter with her uncle at Glenfield.

Fighting for the Right

"I am very glad I was able to do you a good turn, " replied Christy, who considered it his duty to take advantage of the circumstances. "I am just going out to take a sail; won't you join me? "

"Thank you; I shall be very glad to do so. I suppose you are a Yankee still, engaged in the business of subjugating the free South, as I am still a rebel to the backbone, " replied Percy, laughing very pleasantly.

"But you are not in the rebel army now, any more than you were at that time, " added Christy in equally good humor.

"I am not. You know all about my army experience. My brother, the major, sends me a letter by every chance he can get, and has offered to have my indiscretion, as he called it, in leaving the camp, passed over, if I will save the honor of the family by returning to the army; but my father insists that I can render better service to the cause as his assistant. "

Christy led the way down the steps, and the two seated themselves in the bow of the boat. The skipper shoved off after he had set his sails, and the boat stood out towards the Snapper, for he could hardly avoid passing quite near to her.

"What are you doing in Nassau, Christy? " asked Percy.

This was a hard question, and it was utterly impossible to make a truthful reply without upsetting the plan of Mr. Gilfleur, and rendering useless the voyage of the Chateaugay to the Bahamas.

"I am in just as bad a scrape as you were when you were caught on board of the Bellevite, " replied Christy after a moment's reflection.

"Are you a prisoner of war? "

"How could I be a prisoner in a neutral port like Nassau? No; I do not regard myself as a prisoner just now, " answered Christy very good-humoredly.

"But you have been a prisoner, and you have escaped in some vessel that run the blockade. I see it all; and you need not stop to explain it," said Percy, who flattered himself on his brilliant perception.

"The less I say about it the better it will be for me," added Christy, willing to accept the situation as his companion had marked it out.

"But you must not let my father see you."

"I never met Colonel Pierson, though I saw him once, and he would not know me if we should meet."

"Then don't let him know who you are."

"He will not know, unless you tell him."

"You may be very sure that I will not mention you to him, or to anybody else, for that matter," replied Percy very earnestly.

But Christy did not put any confidence in his assertion. Percy was really a deserter from the Confederate army, and he knew that he had in several instances acted the traitor's part. He had more respect for an out-and-out rebel than for one who shirked his duty to his country as he understood it.

"I have been afraid some one might identify me here," suggested Christy, determined not to over-act his part.

"I might help you out of the scrape," said Percy, who appeared to be reflecting upon something that had come to his mind. "I suppose you are aware that most of the vessels in this harbor, and those outside the bar, are directly or indirectly interested in blockade-running."

"I supposed so, but I know nothing about it."

"Some of them have brought in cotton, with which others are loading for England. My business as my father's clerk takes me on board of most of them, and I know the captains and other officers very well. This little steamer we have just passed was bought for a Mobile man by my father. She carried a full cargo of goods into Mobile, and came out again full of cotton. She is called the Snapper, and she is a regular snapper at her business. She is now all loaded, and will sail on the next tide. I am well acquainted with her captain."

"What sort of a man is he?" asked Christy in an indifferent tone.

"He is a very good fellow; bold as an eagle, and brave as a lion. He drinks too much whiskey for his own good; but he knows all the ports on the Gulf of Mexico, and he gets in or out in face of the blockaders every time, " answered Percy with enthusiasm.

"Did he never lose a vessel? "

"Never but one; that was the Floridian, and I reckon you know as much about that affair as any other person, Christy, " replied Percy, laughing as though it had been a good joke on Captain Flanger.

"I know something about it. "

"Your uncle, Colonel Passford, lost several vessels, and you had a hand in their capture. But never mind that; you did me a good turn, and I never go back on a friend. Now, my dear fellow, I do not think it will be safe for you to remain here. You are looked upon as a dangerous fellow along the Gulf coast, as Colonel Passford writes to my father; and if my governor should get a hint that you were here, he would make a business of getting you inside a Confederate prison. "

"I am under the flag of England just now, and that is supposed to protect neutrals. "

"That's all very well, my dear fellow; but my governor could manage your affair in some way. I can make a trade with the captain of the Snapper to put you ashore at Key West. "

"You are very kind, Percy. "

"It will be necessary for you to buy a boat here, one with a sail, which can be carried on the deck of the steamer, " continued Percy, evidently much interested in the scheme he was maturing.

At this moment the Dinah was passing under the stern of a steamer, on which Christy read the name "Ovidio. "

CHAPTER XX

A BAND OF RUFFIANS

The Ovidio was one of the vessels of which Captain Passford had obtained information in New York, and by which the traitor merchant had at first intended to send the machinery on board of the Ionian into the Confederacy.

"That vessel flying the British flag appears to be a man-of-war, " said Christy.

"That is just what she is, confound her! " replied Percy bitterly. "She is the Greyhound, and she has seized the Ovidio which we just passed; but my father believes she will be released; " as in fact she was, after a delay of two months.

"That looks a little like neutrality, " added the naval officer.

"But what do you think of my scheme to get you out of this scrape before you get into any trouble here? " asked Percy, who seemed to his companion to be altogether too much interested in his plan. "Flanger is a friend of mine, for I was able to render him a very important service, nothing less than getting him the command of the Snapper. "

"Of course I want to get out of the scrape. "

"I suppose you haven't money enough to buy the boat, if you escaped from a Confederate prison; but I will help you out on that by lending you forty or fifty dollars. "

"Thank you, Percy, you are behaving like a true friend, and I shall remember you with gratitude, " replied Christy, as earnestly as the occasion seemed to require. "Do you think you can trust Captain Flanger to put me in the way to get to Key West? "

"I am sure I can! " exclaimed the schemer warmly. "He would do anything for me. "

"But perhaps he would not do anything for me. "

Fighting for the Right

"I hope you don't mistrust my sincerity in this matter, my dear fellow, " continued Percy, with an aggrieved expression on his face.

"Oh, no! Certainly not. I only suggested that your friend the captain might not be as willing as you are to let me escape at Key West. "

"I will guarantee his fidelity. I am as sure of him as I am of myself. "

"All right, Percy, I will hold myself subject to your orders. But I think you had better buy the boat, and put it on board of the Snapper, for I could not do so without exposing myself, " suggested Christy. "I have some money that I concealed about me, and I will pay the bills before I go on board of the steamer. "

"I will do everything that is necessary to be done with the greatest pleasure. Perhaps you had better go on board of the Snapper on our return to the town. Then you will not be seen by any person, " suggested Percy with as much indifference as he could assume.

"What time will the steamer sail? "

"About five o'clock, which is high tide. "

"It is only half-past one now; besides, I have to go up to the hotel for my satchel, and to pay my bill. Where do you live, Percy? "

"We have a house on Frederick Street. At what hotel are you stopping? "

"At the Royal Victoria. "

"What is the number of your room? " asked Percy.

"No. 44. "

Christy was sharp enough to comprehend the object of these questions; and, as a matter of precaution, he divided the number of his room by two in making his reply.

"That makes an easy thing of it, " continued Percy. "I will go to the Royal Victoria at four o'clock, pay your bill and get your satchel. I will meet you on the public wharf at half-past, and see that you have a good stateroom in the cabin of the Snapper. "

"That seems to be all very well arranged, " added Christy.

"But I must see Captain Flanger before four o'clock. How much longer do you intend to cruise in this boat? " asked the schemer, beginning to manifest a little impatience.

The conversation had been carried on in a low tone at the bow of the boat, where the boatman could not hear what was said.

"I think I am safer out here than I should be on shore, " suggested Christy. "I might meet some other person in the town who knows me. "

"All right; but I ought to see Captain Flanger as soon as possible, for I shall ask him to buy the boat, " replied Percy uneasily. "You might land me, and then sail another hour or two yourself. "

"Very well; that will suit me exactly. Skipper, this gentleman wishes to be put on shore; but I desire to sail another hour or two, " said Christy, addressing the boatman.

"All right, sir; I will go to the wharf if you say so, but I can put the other gentleman into that boat which has just come over the bar. The boatman is a friend of mine. "

"Who is he, David? " asked Percy.

"Jim Peckson. "

"I know him, and I will go up in his boat if you will hail him, " answered the young Southerner. "I suppose the arrangement is well understood, " he added, dropping his voice so that the boatman could not hear him. "You are to be on the public wharf at half-past four, when I come down with your satchel. "

"Perfectly understood, " added the other.

David hailed his friend Jim Peckson, and Percy was transferred to his boat. Christy felt an intense relief in getting rid of him. Of course he had not the remotest idea of going on board of the Snapper, whose brutal commander had declared that he would kill him. But he realized that Nassau was not a safe place for him.

Fighting for the Right

The boat crossed the bar, and the passenger took his seat by the side of the boatman. David directed his boat towards the larger steamers outside, which were loading with cotton from several small craft. They were, doubtless, to convey it to England. Christy felt no interest in these, for the voyages of the blockade-runners ended when they reached the port of Nassau.

"Shall I sail you over to the sea-gardens now, sir? " asked David, when his passenger intimated that he had seen enough of the vessels outside the bar.

"Yes; anywhere you please, David. I don't care about going on shore before dark, " replied Christy.

The passenger was greatly interested in the sea-gardens, and for more than an hour he gazed through the clear water at the sea-plants on the bottom, and at the many-colored fishes that were swimming about in the midst of them. He was desirous of using up the time until he could have the covert of the friendly darkness. He looked at his watch, and found it was nearly five o'clock.

"What time is it high tide, David? " he asked.

"Five o'clock, sir. "

"Are there any steamers to sail to-day? I suppose they can go over the bar only at full sea. "

"Only small vessels can go over at any other time. The Snapper was to sail at high tide. "

"Then I think we will run down by the light, and see her come out of the harbor, " added Christy.

"I don't believe she will come out this afternoon, sir, " said David.

"Why not? "

"Her captain got arrested for something. I saw four officers taking him to the jail. Some one told me he was drunk, and had pitched into a gentleman who was walking along the sidewalk in front of a saloon on Bay Street. "

"They will discharge him in time to sail on the tide, won't they?"

"I don't reckon they will. The men from the vessels in the harbor at this time make heaps of trouble," replied David. "If the gentleman he hit had a mind to complain of him, the court would lock him up for a week or two."

Christy was not disposed, under the circumstances, to make a complaint. The boat was soon in sight of the lighthouse and the bar. The Dinah made a long stretch to the eastward, and was in sight of the entrance to the harbor till it began to be dark; but no steamer came out on the high tide. The boat crossed the bar again.

"Now, David, I want you to land me some distance beyond the public wharf," said Christy. "How much shall I pay you for this sail?"

"About three dollars, sir, if you don't think that is too much," answered the boatman.

"That is very reasonable for the time you have been out; and there is a sovereign," added the passenger, as he handed him the gold coin.

"I don't think I can change this piece, sir."

"You need not change it; keep the whole of it."

"Oh, thank you, sir! You are very generous, and I thank you with all my heart. I don't often earn that much money in a whole day."

"All right, David; I am satisfied if you are."

"I am more than satisfied, sir. But where shall I land you?"

"I don't know the names of all the streets, but go to the eastward of the public wharf."

"I can land you at the foot of Union Street."

"How will I get to the Royal Victoria Hotel?"

The boatman directed him so that he could find his destination. He was somewhat afraid that Percy Pierson might be on the lookout for the Dinah; but by this time it was so dark that he could hardly make her out. David landed him at the place indicated, and he followed the directions given him, which brought him to the east end of the hotel. It was too early to meet Mr. Gilfleur, and he found the guests were at dinner. He had eaten nothing since the lunch on board of the Eleuthera; and, after he had looked in the faces of all the men at the table, he took his place with them, and did full justice to the fare set before him.

He did not venture to remain in the hotel. He desired to see the detective, for he had decided not to remain another day in Nassau. As long as Percy Pierson was in the town, it was not a safe place for him. He had decided to make his way across the island to the nook where the Eleuthera was concealed, and remain on board of her until the detective returned. But he desired to see him, and report his intention to him, so that he need not be concerned about him.

Christy was entirely satisfied that he had correctly interpreted the purpose of Percy to betray him into the hands of Captain Flanger. As he was not on the public wharf at half-past four, doubtless he had been on the lookout for him. He knew David, and his first step would be to find him. The boatman would be likely to tell him that his fellow-passenger in the Dinah had gone to the hotel. He visited the place arranged for his meeting with Mr. Gilfleur; but it was in advance of the time, and he was not there. He walked about the hotel grounds, careful to avoid every person who came in his way.

In the darkness he saw a man approaching him, and he turned about, walking away in the opposite direction. But presently this person moved off towards the hotel, and he started again for the rendezvous with the detective. He had gone but a short distance before two men sprang upon him, one of them taking him in the rear, and hugging him so that he could not move his arms. He began a mighty struggle; but two more men came out of their hiding-place, and a pair of handcuffs were slipped upon his wrists.

Then he attempted to call for assistance, but a handkerchief was promptly stuffed into his mouth, and the ruffians hurried him out through a narrow gateway to an unfrequented street, where a carriage appeared to be in waiting for them.

"Drive to the beach back of Fort Montague," said one of them.

Fighting for the Right

It was the voice of Captain Flanger.

"Two men sprang upon him."

CHAPTER XXI

A QUESTION OF NEUTRALITY

Even before he heard the voice of his savage enemy, Christy Passford realized that he had fallen into the hands of the commander of the Snapper. He was placed on the back seat of the carriage, with a pair of handcuffs on his wrists, and a handkerchief in his mouth to do duty as a gag. Captain Flanger was at his side, with two other men on the front seat, and one on the box with the driver. Against these four men he was powerless to make any resistance while he was in irons.

The carriage was drawn by two horses, and was considerably larger than the ordinary victoria used in the town. It was quite dark, and though the streets were flanked with many houses, hardly a person appeared to be stirring at this hour. But a vehicle loaded down with the rough visitors of the place could not be an unusual sight, for they were the kind of people who were disposed to make the night hideous, as well as the day.

Christy had struggled with all his might to shake off the ruffians who beset him, and two more had come out from their concealment when he thought he was making some progress in freeing himself from their grasp. As soon as his wrists were ironed he realized that resistance was useless, and that it could only increase his discomfort. It was a terrible calamity to have fallen into the power of a man so brutal and unscrupulous as Captain Flanger, bent upon revenging himself for the mutilation of his most prominent facial member. He was certainly disfigured for life, though the wound made by the ball from the revolver had healed; but it was an ill-looking member, and he appeared to be conscious of his facial deformity all the time.

The men in the carriage said nothing, and Christy way unable to speak. They seemed to be afraid of attracting the attention of the few passers-by in the streets, and of betraying the nature of the outrage in which they were engaged. The streets in the more frequented parts of the town were crowded with men, as the victim had been able to see, and he hoped that they would come across some large collection of people. In that case he decided to make a demonstration that would attract the attention of the police, if nothing more.

He had no idea of the location of Fort Montague, to which the man on the box had been ordered to drive them. The direction was to a beach near the fort; and he had no doubt there would be a boat there in readiness to convey him to the Snapper. But the farther the carriage proceeded, the less frequented the streets became. He found no opportunity to make his intended demonstration. His only hope now was that Mr. Gilfleur, who must have been in the vicinity of the hotel, had witnessed the outrage, and would interfere, as he had done on Bay Street, and save him from the fate that was in store for him.

In a rather lonely place Christy discovered the outline in the darkness of what looked like a fort. At the same moment he heard the distant stroke of some public clock, striking nine o'clock. This was the time appointed for the meeting with the detective, and he had been at the place a quarter of an hour before, which fully explained why the detective had not been there; and probably he had been in his room. This conclusion seemed to cut off all hope that he had witnessed the attack upon him.

The carriage stopped at the beach below the fort. It was the bathing-place for the town, and at this hour it was entirely deserted. The person on the box with the driver was the first to alight, and he ran down to the water. He returned in a few minutes to the carriage, the other ruffians retaining their places.

"The boat is not here yet, but it is coming, " said this man, reporting to the captain.

"All right; I told the mate to be here at nine o'clock, and it has just struck that hour, " replied Flanger. "Go down to the water, driver. "

The vehicle moved down to the water's edge and stopped again. At the same time the boat grated on the sand, and came to a halt a few feet from the dry ground.

"We are all right now, " said the person who had been with the driver on the box; and this time Christy recognized his voice as that of Percy Pierson.

He had not mistaken or misjudged him. He had not been able to understand why the young man should befriend him, and it was clear enough now, if it had not been before, that his gratitude towards him was a mere pretence. Captain Passford, senior desired to get rid of him, and had put him on board of the schooner for this reason only.

"Captain Passford, we meet again, as I was sure we should when we parted in Nassau to-day, " said the commander of the Snapper. "Now, if you will take the trouble to get out of the carriage, we shall be able to make you comfortable before we have done with you. "

Christy attempted to speak; but the gag prevented him from articulating, and he could not breathe as freely as usual. The captain drew the handkerchief from his mouth, for there was no one within a long distance of the spot to aid the prisoner if he had called for help. The victim had fully determined to resign himself to his fate, and make the best of the situation until an opportunity offered to effect his escape, though he greatly feared that such an opportunity would not be presented.

"Thank you, Captain Flanger; I am much obliged to you for giving me a better chance to breathe, though I suppose you are not very anxious that I should continue to breathe, " replied Christy, assuming a degree of good nature which had no substantial foundation in reality. "On the contrary, I dare say you intend to stop my breathing altogether as soon as you find it convenient to do so. "

"Not so; you can do all the breathing you want to, and I won't interfere as long as you behave yourself, " replied Captain Flanger in a more civilized tone than his victim had heard him use before.

"But to-day noon you swore that you would kill me, " added the prisoner, much surprised at the change in the manner of the ruffian since they had met on the sidewalk.

"I have altered my mind, " replied the captain, leaving Christy in the hands of his companions, and walking down to the boat, where the two men in it seemed to be trying to find deeper water, so as to bring it nearer to the shore.

"Well, how do you find yourself, Christy? " asked Percy, placing himself in front of him.

"I haven't lost myself so far, and I am as comfortable as could be expected under the circumstances, " answered Christy, whose pride would not permit him to show that he was overcome or cast down by the misfortune which had overtaken him.

"You did not come to the public wharf as you promised to do at half-past four o'clock this afternoon, " Percy proceeded.

"I did not; David sailed me off to the sea-gardens, and we did not get back to the town in season for me to keep the appointment. "

"Then you intended to keep it? "

"I did not say so. "

"I had the idea you were a fellow that kept all the promises he made, even if it hurt him to do so. "

"Do you think you would have kept your promise to have Captain Flanger land me at Key West, if I had been weak enough to go on board of his steamer? " demanded Christy.

"You are fighting on one side, and I am fighting on the other, Christy; and I suppose either of us is justified in lying and breaking his promises in the service of his country. "

"You are fighting on your side at a very convenient distance from the battle-ground, Percy. "

"I am fighting here because I can render the best service to my country in this particular place, " replied the young Southerner with spirit. "I am sure I could not do anything better for my country than send you back to the Confederate prison from which you escaped. "

"Even if you violate the neutrality of the place, " suggested Christy. "The British government was ready to declare war against the United States when a couple of Confederate commissioners were taken out of an English steamer by a man-of-war. Do you suppose that when this outrage is known, England will not demand reparation, even to the restoring of the victim to his original position on this island? I hope you have considered the consequences of this violation of the neutrality of the place. "

"I don't bother my head about matters of that sort. I have talked about it with my father, and I think he understands himself, " replied Percy very flippantly.

"I don't think he does. I have the same rights in Nassau that you and your father possess. You are carrying on the war on neutral ground; and no nation would permit that. "

"I am no lawyer, Christy. I only know that you have done a great deal of mischief to our cause in the Gulf, as set forth in the letters of your uncle to my father. "

"But I have fought my battles in the enemy's country, or on the open sea; and I have not done it while skulking under a neutral flag, " replied the naval officer, with quite as much spirit as his adversary in the debate. "You and Captain Flanger, with the co-operation of your father, it appears, are engaged in a flagrant outrage against the sovereignty of England. "

"My father has nothing to do with it; I will take back what I said about him, " added Percy, evidently alarmed at the strength of the argument against him.

"You told me that you had talked with your father about the case. "

"But I withdraw that statement; he knows nothing about it. "

"You make two diametrically opposite statements; and I am justified in accepting the one that suits me best as the truth. If Captain Flanger does not hang me to the yard-arm as soon as he gets me into blue water, I shall make my complaint to the United States government as soon as I have an opportunity to do so; and I have no doubt you and your father will have permission to leave Nassau, never to return. "

Percy was silent, and appeared to be in deep thought. Captain Flanger had returned to the spot from the boat, and had listened to the last part of the discussion.

"Captain Flanger understands enough of international law to see that I am right, " continued Christy, when Percy made no reply.

"The people here treat us very handsomely, my little larky, " said Captain Flanger, with a coarse laugh. "I am not to be scared out of my game by any such bugbears as you talk about. But I am willing to say this, my little rooster: I have no intention to hang you to the yard-arm, as you hinted that I might."

"At noon to-day you swore that you would kill me."

"I have altered my mind, as I told you before," growled the commander of the Snapper, with very ill grace, as though he was ashamed because he had abandoned his purpose to commit a murder. "I am not what you call a temperance man; and when I get ashore, and in good company, I sometimes take a little more good whiskey than it is prudent; but I don't drink anything on board of my ship. To cut it short, I was a little too much in the wind when I said I was going to kill you. I am sober now."

"I think you must be able to see what the consequences of murdering a person captured on British soil would be, Captain Flanger," suggested Christy.

"As I have told you twice before, I do not intend to murder you," said the captain angrily. "I am going to put you back in the prison from which you escaped; that's all. No more talk; take him to the boat."

The two men at Christy's side marched him down to the boat, and seated him in the stern. The rest of the party took places, and shoved off. In half an hour the boat was alongside the Snapper.

CHAPTER XXII

ON BOARD OF THE SNAPPER

Christy could not help seeing that a great change had come over the manner of Captain Flanger, especially in his repeated declarations that he did not intend to kill his prisoner. His thirst for revenge could hardly have abated as the effect of his cups passed off, and it was evident to the victim of the outrage that some other influence had been brought to bear upon him. It did not seem possible to him that Percy Pierson could have modified his vindictive nature to this degree.

The young man's father could not fail to see the peril of the step his son was taking, though he appeared not to have been able to resist the temptation to get rid of such an active enemy as Christy had proved himself to be. It looked plain enough to the victim, as he considered the situation, that Colonel Pierson's influence had produced the change in the intentions of Captain Flanger. If the prisoner were brutally treated, and especially if his life were taken, it would make the breach of neutrality so much the more flagrant.

"Help the young cub on board, " said the captain, as he went up the accommodation ladder, followed by Percy.

With his wrists fettered with a pair of handcuffs, Christy needed assistance to mount the vessel's side. He was handled with more consideration than he expected, and reached the deck without any injury. By the order of the captain he was conducted to the cabin, where he seated himself on a stool near the companion-way. A few minutes later Percy came down the steps with a valise in his hand, which he deposited in one of the staterooms.

"I am your fellow-passenger, Christy, " said he, when he came out of the room. "I hope we shall be good friends. "

"After the treachery which has been practised upon me to-day, there cannot be much love wasted between us, though I am not disposed to be a bear, even under the present unfavorable circumstances, " replied the prisoner. "I suppose this steamer is to run the blockade? "

Fighting for the Right

"Of course she is to run the blockade; how else could she get into Mobile?" replied Percy.

"You can bet your worthless life she is going to run the blockade, and you may be sure that she will get in too," added Captain Flanger, who came into the cabin at the moment the question was asked.

"By the way, Christy, from what prison in the Confederacy did you make your escape?"

"If you will excuse me, I prefer to answer no questions."

"Just as you please, my boy. We shall know all about it when we get to Mobile," said Percy lightly. "I am going home for a few days to see my mother, who is in feeble health. I don't want to quarrel with you; and if I can be of any service to you after we get into port, I shall be happy to do so. We sail at about five o'clock in the morning, on the high tide."

"Captain Passford," began the commander, in a more subdued tone than the prisoner had ever heard him use.

"That title does not apply to me now, Captain Flanger," Christy interposed. "If I ever get back to my duty on shipboard, it will be as second lieutenant of the Bellevite."

"Mr. Passford, if that suits you better, I was going to say that I mean to treat you like a gentleman, whether you are one or not, in spite of my shattered and battered nose," added the captain.

"I do not consider myself responsible for the condition of your nose, Captain Flanger. At the time you received that wound you were engaged in a daring adventure, with two revolvers in your hands, ready to blow my brains out. It was war, and I did nothing but my plain duty; and even in a time of peace I had the natural right to defend myself, and save my own life, even at the sacrifice of yours, as you were the assailant," argued Christy quite warmly. "You would have put a ball through my head or heart if I had not fired at the moment I did."

"Why didn't you shoot me like a gentleman, and not blow my nose off?" demanded the captain bitterly.

Fighting for the Right

"I had to fire in a hurry; and I did not aim at your nose. I could only discharge my weapon on the instant, and I had no time to aim at any particular part of you. I intended simply to cover your head."

"But you blowed my nose off all the same."

"I had no grudge against your nose. Do you think it would be honorable for a soldier to revenge himself on neutral ground for a wound received in the field?"

"But it was a sneaking Yankee trick to shoot at a man's nose, even in a square battle by sea or by land," protested the captain with a rattling oath.

It was useless to discuss the matter with such a man, though he had probably been charged by Colonel Pierson not to do his prisoner any injury, and Christy relapsed into silence.

"If you propose to treat me like a gentleman, whether I am one or not, may I ask where you propose to berth me, for I am very much fatigued to-night?" asked the prisoner later in the evening.

"I mean to give you as good a stateroom as I have myself; but it will contain two berths, and the mate will occupy the lower one, to prevent you from escaping, if you should take it into your head to do so," replied the captain, as he opened the door of one of the rooms.

"I can hardly get into the upper berth with my wrists ironed," said the prisoner, exhibiting his fetters.

"That is so," replied the captain, taking the key of the manacles from his pocket and removing them. "But I warn you that any attempt to escape may get you into a worse scrape than you are in now. When we get to sea you shall have your liberty."

"Thank you, Captain, for this indulgence. I suppose you will not make a long voyage of it to Mobile. I presume you go to the northward of Great Abaco Island?" asked Christy, though he hardly expected to receive an answer to his question.

"Why do you presume such a stupid idea as that?" demanded the captain, who seemed to regard the inquiry as an imputation upon his seamanship; and the inquirer had put the question to provoke an answer. "I have been sailing nearly all my life in these waters, and I know where I am. Why should I add three hundred miles to my voyage when there is no reason for it? "

"I am not much acquainted down here. "

"I shall go through the North-west, or Providence Channel. "

Captain Flanger did not know that the steamer Chateaugay was cruising somewhere in the vicinity of the Bahamas; but his prisoner did know it, and the information given him was not pleasant or satisfactory. Captain Chantor had told him that he intended to stand off and to the eastward of Great Abaco, and he had been cherishing a hope that he would fall in with the Snapper, though he might not find evidence enough on board of her to warrant her capture.

If he fell in with the steamer, he would be likely to examine her; and that would lead to the release of the involuntary passenger. But if the Snapper went through the Providence Channel, the Chateaugay would not be likely to fall in with her. It looked to the unfortunate officer as though he was booked for a rebel prison. He could see no hope of escape, though he was duly grateful for the change which had come over his vicious persecutor. If he was allowed his liberty, he might find some avenue of escape open. It was useless to groan over his fate, and he did not groan; but he had come to the conclusion that it would be a long time before he took possession of his stateroom in the ward room of the Bellevite.

Availing himself of the permission given to him, he went into the room, and turned in with his clothes on, so that he might be in readiness for any event. Mr. Gilfleur would miss him at the rendezvous agreed upon; but he would have no means of knowing that anything had happened to him. Tired as he was, he was not inclined to sleep. Presently he heard a conversation which was not intended for his ears, for it was carried on in very low tones.

"Do you know, Captain Flanger, that I believe we are getting into a very bad scrape? " said Percy Pierson in a subdued tone.

"What are you afraid of? " demanded the captain, in a voice hardly above a whisper.

"My father refused at first to permit the capture of Passford," added Percy. "He would consent to it only after you had promised to treat him well."

"I am treating him as well as I know how, though it goes against my grain. We will get him into the jail in Mobile, and keep him there till the Yankees have acknowledged the independence of the Confederacy, and paid for all the damage they have done to our country. How is any one in Washington or London to know anything about this little affair of to-night?"

"I don't know how; but if it should get out, the Yankees would make an awful row, and England would be obliged to do something about it."

"But we must make sure that it does not get out. The young cub has a deal of spirit and pluck, and he would not live long if he were shut up on such rations as our men have."

Percy seemed to be better satisfied than he had been, and the conversation turned to other subjects in which the listener had no interest. Without much of an effort he turned over and went to sleep. When he woke in the morning he heard the tramp of footsteps on the deck over his head, and he concluded that the steamer was getting under way. If the mate had slept in the berth below him, he had not seen or heard him. He leaped out of the bed, and descended to the floor. When he tried the door he found that it was locked.

Presently he heard the movement of the screw, and felt the motion of the vessel. There was a port light to the room, and he placed himself where he could see out at it. But there was nothing to be seen which afforded him any hope of comfort. There must be a pilot on board, and he began to wonder if there could be any way to communicate with him. He took from his pocket a piece of paper and pencil. He wrote a brief statement of the outrage which had been perpetrated upon him, folded the paper, and put it in his vest pocket, where he could readily slip it into the hand of the pilot, if he found the opportunity to do so. The captain had promised to give him his liberty when the vessel got out to sea, and he hoped to be able to go on deck before the pilot left the steamer.

The Snapper continued to go ahead, and in a short time she made a sort of a plunge, as she went over the bar. The motion of the steamer began to be rather violent, and Christy saw through the port the white caps that indicated a strong north-west wind. When the vessel had continued on her course for a couple of hours, she stopped, and the prisoner saw the pilot boat drop astern a little later. The opportunity to deliver his statement had passed by, and he tore up the paper, keeping the fragments in his pocket, so that they should not expose his intention.

He had scarcely destroyed the paper before his door was thrown open by Percy Pierson, who informed him that he was at liberty to go on deck if he wished to do so. He accepted the permission. He could see the land in the distance in several directions, but he had no interest in anything. He was called to breakfast soon after, and he took a hearty meal, for the situation had not yet affected his appetite. In the middle of the forenoon, with the light at Hole in the Wall on the starboard, and that on Stirrup Cay on the port, the course of the Snapper was changed to the north-west.

At this point Christy discovered a three-masted steamer, which had also excited the attention of Captain Flanger. It looked like the Chateaugay; and the prisoner's heart bounded with emotion.

CHAPTER XXIII

THE CHATEAUGAY IN THE DISTANCE

The steamer which Christy had discovered was a long distance from the Snapper. She had just come about, and this movement had enabled the prisoner to see that she had three masts; but that was really all there was to lead him to suppose she was the Chateaugay. She was too far off for him to make her out; and if he had not known that she was cruising to the eastward of the Bahamas, it would not have occurred to him that she was the steamer in which he had been a passenger two days before.

Captain Flanger discovered the sail a few minutes later, and fixed his attention upon it. In the business in which he was engaged it was necessary to practise the most unceasing vigilance. But, at this distance from any Confederate port, the commander of the steamer did not appear to be greatly disturbed at the sight of a distant sail, believing that his danger was nearer the shores of the Southern States. Doubtless he had papers of some sort which would show that his vessel had cleared for Havana, or some port on the Gulf of Mexico.

Christy did not deem it wise to manifest any interest in the distant sail, and, fixing his gaze upon the deck-planks, he continued to walk back and forth, as he was doing when he discovered the steamer. He had not been able to make out her course. He had first seen her when she was in the act of turning, obtaining only a glance at the three masts. Whether or not she was "end-on" for the Snapper, he could not determine, and Captain Flanger seemed to be studying up this question with no little earnestness.

The principal mission in these waters of the Chateaugay was to look up the Ovidio, of which Captain Passford in New York had obtained some information through his agents. This vessel was not simply a blockade-runner, but was intended for a cruiser, though she had sailed from Scotland without an armament. It was known that she would proceed to Nassau, and this fact had suggested to Mr. Gilfleur his visit to that port to obtain reliable information in regard to her, as well as incidentally to look into the methods of fitting out vessels for running the blockade.

Fighting for the Right

Captain Chantor was expecting to fall in with the Ovidio, even before the return of his two passengers. He did not believe the authorities at Nassau would permit her to take on board an armament at that port; but a rendezvous had probably been arranged, where she was to receive her guns and ammunition. But the only safe channel for any vessel to get to the deep sea from Nassau was by the one that had received the name of Providence. This channel is a continuation of what is called "The Tongue of the Ocean, " which extends over a hundred miles south of New Providence, a hundred and fifty fathoms in depth, and bordered by innumerable cays, reefs, and very shoal water.

South of Great Abaco Island, this channel, from thirty to forty miles wide, divides into the North-east and North-west Channels, and all vessels of any great draught can safely get out to sea only through one of them. It was evident enough to Captain Chantor, who was familiar with the navigation of these seas, that the Ovidio must come out through one of the channels indicated. Christy had talked with the commander of the Chateaugay in regard to these passages, and knew that it was his intention to keep a close watch over them.

He could not be sure that the steamer in the distance was the Chateaugay; but the more he recalled what had passed between himself and Captain Chantor, and considered the situation, the stronger became his hope that it was she. He was sure that she had come about, and he reasoned that she had done so when her commander ascertained that the steamer he had sighted laid her course through the North-west Channel. This was as far as he could carry his speculations.

Without understanding the situation as well as did his prisoner, Captain Flanger seemed to be nervous and uneasy. He watched the distant sail for a long time, sent for his spy-glass and examined her, and then began to plank the deck. When he came abreast of Christy he stopped.

"Do you see that sail off to the eastward, Mr. Passford? "

"I see it now, Captain, " replied the prisoner, as indifferently as possible, for he felt that it would be very imprudent to manifest any interest in the matter.

"Can you make out what she is? " continued the captain.

"I cannot; she must be eight or ten miles from us, " replied Christy, as he glanced to the eastward.

"I shouldn't wonder if that was one of your Yankee gunboats, " added Captain Flanger, spicing his remark with a heavy oath, for he could hardly say anything without interlarding his speech with profanity.

"It may be, for aught I know, " replied the prisoner with something like a yawn.

"Whatever she is, the Snapper can run away from her, and you need not flatter yourself that there is any chance for you to escape from a Confederate prison; and when they get you into it, they will hold on very tight. "

"I must take things as they come, " added Christy.

He wanted to ask the captain why he wondered if the sail was a Yankee gunboat, but he did not think it would be prudent to do so. The captain seemed to have, or pretended to have, great confidence in the speed of the Snapper. When he left his prisoner he went to the engine-room, and it was soon evident from the jar and shake of the vessel that he had instructed the chief engineer to increase the speed.

Christy watched the distant sail for about three hours before he could come to any conclusion. At the end of this time he was satisfied that the three-masted steamer was gaining very decidedly upon the Snapper. He began to cherish a very lively hope that the sail would prove to be the Chateaugay. Captain Flanger remained on deck all the forenoon, and every hour that elapsed found him more nervous and excitable.

"I reckon that's a Yankee gunboat astern of us, Mr. Passford; but I am going to get away from her, " said the captain, as they sat down to dinner.

"Is she gaining upon you, Captain? " asked Christy.

"I don't think she is; but if she does get any nearer to us, I shall give her the slip. The Snapper is going into Mobile Bay as sure as you live. You can bet your life on it, " insisted the captain.

Christy was not disposed to converse on the subject, and he began to wonder in what manner the Snapper could give her pursuer the slip. The former was the smaller vessel, and probably did not draw over fourteen feet of water, if she did more than twelve. It might be possible for her to run into shoal water where the pursuer could not follow her.

After the dinner table was cleared off, the captain seated himself at it with a chart spread out before him. It was plain enough that he was devising some expedient to escape the three-master. Christy did not deem it prudent to observe him, and he went on deck. It was as clear as the daylight that the pursuer was gaining rapidly upon the Snapper; and the prisoner did not believe that the latter was making over twelve knots.

By this time seven hours had elapsed since the distant sail had come in sight, and she was now near enough for the prisoner to be sure that she was the Chateaugay. She could make sixteen knots when driven at her best, and she must be gaining four or five knots an hour on the chase. Christy had been through this channel in the Bellevite, and he discovered that the steamer was running near the shoal water. Presently the captain came on deck, and he appeared to be less nervous than before, perhaps because he had arranged his plan to escape his pursuer.

Within an hour Christy recognized the East Isaac, a rock rising ten or twelve feet above the surface of the water, which he identified by its nearness to one over which the sea was breaking. The captain was too much occupied in the study of the surroundings to take any notice of him, and he endeavored to keep out of his sight.

The prisoner consulted his watch, and found it was four o'clock. The tower of the Great Isaac light could just be made out. The Chateaugay was not more than four miles astern of the Snapper, and in another hour she would certainly come up with her, if Captain Flanger did not put his plan into execution. The course of the chase continued to bring her nearer to the reefs.

"Ring one bell!" shouted the captain to the quartermaster at the wheel.

The effect of one bell was to reduce the speed of the Snapper by one-half. The order to put the helm hard a starboard followed in a short time. The course was made about south, and the steamer went ahead slowly. Two men in the chains were heaving the lead constantly. They were reporting four and five fathoms. After the vessel had gone five or six miles on this course, it was changed to about southwest. She was then moving in a direction directly opposite to that of the Chateaugay, and the anxious prisoner could see the man-of-war across the reefs which lifted their heads above the water, very nearly abreast of the Snapper, though at least ten miles distant from her.

"Do you know what steamer that is, Mr. Passford? " asked Captain Flanger, coming aft, apparently for the purpose of finding him.

"How should I know, Captain? " asked Christy.

"I thought you might know her by sight. "

"I could hardly be expected to know all the ships in the United States navy by sight, Captain, for there are a great many of them by this time. "

"All right; she looks like a pretty large vessel, and the bigger the better. I hope you won't get up a disappointment for yourself by expecting that you are going to get out of this scrape, " said Captain Flanger, and there was a great deal of bitterness in his tones.

"I am taking things as they come, Captain. "

"The Snapper is not a man-of-war, and she is engaged in a peaceful voyage. If that fellow thinks of capturing me, he is reckoning without his host. He has no more right to make a prize of me than he has to murder me, " protested the captain, as he gave the order to hoist the British flag.

"Of course you know your business better than I do, Captain Flanger, and I don't propose to interfere with it, " replied Christy.

The commander walked forward again, giving the order to the quartermaster to ring two bells, which presently brought the steamer to a full stop, quite near the rocks which were awash to the northward of her. As the captain moved forward he encountered the first officer in the waist, who addressed him, and they began a conversation, none of which Christy could hear. From the looks and gestures of the mate, he concluded that they were talking about him.

It was not difficult to imagine the subject of the conversation, and it was evident to Christy that the first officer had suggested an idea to his commander. While he was waiting impatiently to ascertain what the Chateaugay would do next, Percy Pierson came on deck looking very pale, for it had been reported at breakfast that he was very sea-sick.

"How are you, Christy? " asked the Southerner.

"I am very well, I thank you. "

"Haven't you been sea-sick? " asked the invalid.

"Of course not; I never was sea-sick. "

"But what has the steamer stopped for? " asked Percy, looking about him.

"Captain Flanger seems to think that vessel over there is a United States man-of-war. "

"Will she capture the Snapper? " asked the sufferer, looking paler than before.

At this moment a boat was lowered from the davits into the water, and Christy was invited by the mate to take a seat in the stern sheets. He was astounded at this request, and wondered what it meant.

CHAPTER XXIV

THE TABLES TURNED

Christy understood the character of Captain Flanger well enough to be confident he meant mischief to him in getting him into the boat. He concluded that this movement was the result of the conference with the mate. He had a suspicion that his terrible enemy intended to drown him, or get rid of him in some other manner.

"May I ask where I am to be taken in the boat, Mr. Dawbin? " asked the prisoner, suppressing as much as he could the excitement that disturbed him.

"I give you leave to ask, but I cannot answer you, " replied the mate.

"If you intend to put me on board of that steamer, it can do no harm to say so, I think, " added Christy.

"If you will excuse me, Mr. Passford, I cannot answer any questions. I ask you again to get into the boat, " said Mr. Dawbin.

"Well, sir, suppose I decline to do so? "

"Then I shall be compelled to use force, and tumble you into the boat in the best way I can, with the assistance of my men. "

"If you intend to murder me, why can't you do the deed here on deck? " demanded the prisoner.

"I don't intend to murder you. "

"That is some consolation. That lighthouse on the Great Isaac is the only place to which you can convey me, and that is sixteen miles from this steamer. I can't believe you intend to pull me that distance."

"No fooling there! " shouted the captain. "What are you waiting for, Mr. Dawbin? Why don't you obey my order? "

"The fellow wants to talk, " replied the mate.

Fighting for the Right

"If he won't get into the boat, pitch him into it like a dead dog!"

Christy saw that it was useless to resist, though he had a revolver in his pocket which had not been taken from him, for he had not been searched. The mate and two sailors stood in front of him, and he realized that he could accomplish nothing by resistance under present circumstances. He thought he could do better in the boat after it was beyond the reach of any reinforcements from the steamer. He went over the side, and took his place in the stern sheets.

The mate followed him, and the two men, one of whom was hardly more than a boy, took their places on the thwarts. The boat was shoved off, and the prisoner had an immediate interest in the course it was about to steer. The mate arranged the tiller lines, and then looked about him.

He directed his gaze towards the north, and seemed to be trying to find some object or point. He satisfied himself in some manner, and then resumed his seat, from which he had risen in order to obtain a better view over the waves. The passenger had watched him closely, and found that his vision had been directed towards the rocks awash and the East Isaac rock. Towards these objects he steered the boat. The Chateaugay was at least three miles to the eastward of these rocks.

Christy watched the course of the boat long enough to satisfy himself that it was headed for the rocks, which were awash at high tide, though they now looked like a minute island. There could be but one object in visiting this locality: and that must be to leave him on that desolate reef. The wind was still fresh from the north-west, and the spray was dashed over the rocks in a manner which suggested that a human being could not remain long on it after the tide was high without being washed off. It was little better than murder to leave him there, and he knew very well that Captain Flanger would shed no tears if assured that his troublesome prisoner was no more.

Christy decided that he would not be left on the reef, or even on the top of the East Isaac, which might be a drier place, though hardly more comfortable. It must have been Mr. Dawbin who had suggested the idea of landing him on the reef, for there was no other place nearer than the Great Isaac light. Captain Flanger had boasted that he sailed a vessel on a peaceful mission, and that the commander of the Chateaugay had no more right to capture him than he had to murder him. But the prisoner knew that the Snapper was to run the blockade, and was bound to Mobile, for the captain had told him so himself.

The commander could now see the folly of his boast. He had not expected to encounter a United States man-of-war in the Bahamas. His prisoner was a naval officer, and would be a strong witness against him. Upon his testimony, and such other evidence as the cargo and other circumstances might supply, the captain of the steamer in the channel might feel justified in making a prize of the Snapper. It was necessary, therefore, to remove this witness against him. As Christy had imagined, the captain had not thought of his prisoner as a witness, and the mate had suggested it to him.

"I suppose I need not ask you what is to be done with me, for that is sufficiently apparent now, " said Christy, more to engage the attention of the mate than for any other reason.

"You can form your own conclusion, " replied Mr. Dawbin.

"You intend to leave me on that reef ahead, and doubtless you expect me to be washed off and drowned, or starved to death there," added the prisoner. "I can't see why you take all this trouble when you could more conveniently blow my brains out. "

"The captain has promised not to harm you, Mr. Passford, and he will keep his word, " replied the mate with very ill grace.

"I consider it worse than murder to leave me on that reef, or any of these rocks, Mr. Dawbin. Since I understand your intention, I might as well put a bullet through my own head, and save myself from all the suffering in store for me, " said Christy, assuming the manner of one rendered desperate by his situation. "Have you a revolver in your pocket? "

"I have not a revolver in my pocket; and if I had I should not lend it to you to shoot yourself, " replied the mate.

Mr. Dawbin had no revolver in his pocket, and that was all the prisoner had been driving at. He was equally confident that neither of the sailors was armed, for he had looked them over to see if there was any appearance of pistols in their pockets.

"You are making altogether too much fuss over this little matter, Mr. Passford. The captain desires you to remain on one of these rocks till he gets through his business with the commander of that steamer in the channel, which is now headed for the Snapper," the mate explained. "When that is finished we will take you off and proceed on our voyage."

"You had better put a bullet through my head."

"I don't think so. It is no great hardship for you to stay a few hours on that rock. You have had your dinner, and you will not starve to death. I don't think you will have to stay there long, for that steamer draws too much water to come in among these reefs, and she will be hard and fast on one of the shoals before she goes much farther."

"Possibly her captain knows what he is about as well as you do," suggested Christy.

"I don't believe he does. There isn't a fathom of water on some of these shoals."

But the Chateaugay kept on her course, though she proceeded very slowly. When she was off the Gingerbread Cay she stopped her screw, and she was near enough for the observer to see that she was lowering at least two boats into the water. In a few minutes more they were seen pulling towards the Snapper, whose boat was now very near the reef which had been selected as the prisoner's abiding-place. A few minutes later the keel ground on the coral rock.

"Jump ashore, both of you, and take the painter with you, my men," said the mate, when the boat stuck about six feet from the top of the ledge.

The two sailors waded to the highest part of the reef, and began to haul in on the painter; but they could not get it anything less than three feet from the rock.

"We can't get the boat any nearer, Mr. Passford; but you are a vigorous young man, and you can easily leap to the rock," said Mr. Dawbin.

"Do you think you could leap to the ledge?" asked Christy, looking him sharp in the eye.

"I know I could."

"Let me see you try it, Mr. Dawbin," replied Christy, with his right hand on his revolver.

"Come, come! Mr. Passford. No fooling. I have no time to spare," growled the mate.

"I am not fooling. As you consider it no hardship to pass a few hours on that rock, I am going to trouble you to take my place there."

"No nonsense! I am not to be trifled with!"

"Neither am I," added the prisoner, as he drew out his weapon, and aimed it at the head of the mate. "You can take your choice between the rock and a ball from my revolver, Mr. Dawbin."

"Do you mean to murder me?" demanded the mate.

"I hope you will not compel me to do so harsh a thing as that. But no fooling! I have no time to spare. Jump on the rock, or I will fire before you are ten seconds older!" said Christy resolutely.

"Come back into the boat, men!" shouted the officer.

"The first one that comes any nearer the boat is a dead man!" added the prisoner, "Five seconds gone, Mr. Dawbin."

The mate did not wait for anything more, but made the leap to the rock. He accomplished it so hastily that he fell when he struck the ledge; but the impetus he had given the boat forced it from the rock, and sent it a considerable distance. Christy restored the revolver to his pocket, and, taking one of the oars, he sculled towards the Chateaugay, which was now much nearer than the Snapper. The two boats from the man-of-war took no notice of him, and perhaps did not see him.

Taking out his white handkerchief he attached it to the blade of one of the oars, and waved it with all his might in the direction of the steamer. He set it up in the mast-hole through the forward thwart, and then continued to scull. But his signal was soon seen, and a boat came off from the steamer.

"Jump on the rock or I will fire before you are ten seconds older."

"Boat ahoy!" shouted the officer in charge of the cutter.

"In the boat!" replied Christy, turning around as he suspended his labor with the oar.

"Lieutenant Passford!" exclaimed Mr. Hackling, the second lieutenant of the Chateaugay. "Is it possible that it is you?"

"I haven't any doubt of it, Mr. Hackling, if you have," replied the late prisoner, heartily rejoiced to find himself in good company again.

"But what does this mean? How do you happen to be here?" demanded the astonished lieutenant of the ship.

"I happen to be here because I have just played a sharp game. I was a prisoner on that steamer yonder, on my way to a rebel prison. But I think it is necessary that I should report immediately to Captain Chantor in regard to the character of the Snapper, which is the name of the vessel you have been chasing."

The Snapper's boat was taken in tow, and the crew of the cutter gave way with a will. In due time Christy was received with the most unbounded astonishment by the commander on the deck of the Chateaugay.

"Where is Mr. Gilfleur? I hope that no accident has happened to him," said the captain with deep anxiety on his face.

"None that I am aware of; but if you will excuse me from explanations for the present, I will state that the steamer on the bank is the Snapper, Captain Flanger, bound for Mobile; and the captain told me that he intended to run the blockade."

"Mr. Hackling, take charge of the second cutter, and give Mr. Birdwing my order to make a prize of that steamer, and bring her off to the deep water."

It was quite dark when this order was executed.

CHAPTER XXV

CAPTAIN FLANGER IN IRONS

Christy Passford related to Captain Chantor all that had occurred to the detective and himself from the time of their departure from the ship to their parting on the shore; and he did not fail to mention the fact that Mr. Gilfleur had come to his assistance when he was assaulted by the ruffian in front of the saloon.

"You have had a narrow escape, Mr. Passford, " said the commander, when he had concluded. "The idea of avenging an injury received in that way is something I never happened to hear of before, though my experience is not unlimited. Mr. Birdwing, " he continued, after the first lieutenant had reported to him, "had you any difficulty in effecting the capture of the Snapper? "

"Only with the captain; for my force was sufficient to have taken her if she had been fully armed and manned. There was no fighting; but I was obliged to put the captain in irons, for he was about the ugliest and most unreasonable man I ever encountered, " replied the chief of the boat expedition. "I was not at all satisfied that the steamer was a fit subject for capture till your order came to me, brought by Mr. Hackling. Then Captain Flanger not only protested, with more bad language than I ever before heard in the same time, but he absolutely refused to yield. I could not give him the reasons that induced you to send me the order, and I referred the matter to you. "

The Snapper had been anchored within a cable's length of the Chateaugay, and Mr. Birdwing had brought Captain Flanger on board of the ship, with Percy Pierson, that the question of prize might be definitely settled by the commander, for he was not quite satisfied himself. The captain of the Snapper was still in irons, and he and his companion had been put under guard in the waist. The man with the mutilated nose had not yet seen Christy, and possibly he was still wondering what had become of his chief officer and the two men who had been ordered to put the prisoner on the ledge.

Christy had informed Captain Chantor, in his narrative, of the manner in which he had turned the tables on his custodians, and he had not forgotten that the party were still where he had left them. He reminded the commander of the latter fact, and a quartermaster was sent in the third cutter to bring them off, and put them on board of the Snapper; where a considerable force still remained under the charge of Mr. Carlin, the third lieutenant.

"Now we will settle this matter with the captain of the Snapper, and I hope to convince him that his vessel is a lawful prize, so far as she can be so declared in advance of the decision of the court, " said Captain Chantor. "Come with me, if you please, Mr. Birdwing. For the present, Mr. Passford, will you oblige me by keeping in the shade till I send for you? "

"Certainly, Captain Chantor, though I should like to hear what Captain Flanger has to say in defence of his steamer, " replied the passenger. "But I will take care not to show myself to him till you are ready for me. "

"I do not object to that arrangement. I do not quite understand who this Percy Pierson is, though you mentioned him in your report of what had occurred during your absence, " added the commander.

"He is the son of Colonel Richard Pierson, a Confederate commissioner, who represents his government at Nassau, purchasing vessels as opportunity to do so is found. His son is the person who tried to induce me to take passage in the Snapper, with the promise that I should be permitted to land at Key West. It was only a trick to get me on board of the steamer; and when it failed, for I declined to fall into the trap, I was captured by a gang of four or five ruffians, Captain Flanger being one of them, and conveyed to the vessel, where I was locked up in a stateroom till after she had sailed. "

"That is a proper question for the British government to deal with, and I hope it will be put in the way of adjustment by the proper officials, though I am inclined to regard it as an act of war, which will justify me in holding the men engaged in the outrage as prisoners. Do you know who they are, Mr. Passford? "

"I can designate only three of them, —the captain, Mr. Dawbin, the mate, who is now on the ledge, and Percy Pierson. I am sure they were all in the carriage that conveyed me to the beach where I was put into the boat. The others were sailors, and I could not identify them. "

Fighting for the Right

"I will hold the three you name as prisoners, " added Captain Chantor, as he moved forward, followed by the executive officer.

It was getting dark, and Christy made his way to the shadow of the mainmast, where he obtained a position that enabled him to hear all that passed without being seen himself. Captain Flanger seemed to be more subdued than he had been reported to be on board of the Snapper, and the commander ordered the irons to be taken from his wrists.

"Captain Flanger, I have concluded to make a prize of the Snapper; but I am willing to hear anything you may wish to offer, " Captain Chantor began.

"I protest; you have no more right to make a prize of my vessel than you have to capture a British man-of-war, if you were able to do such a thing, " replied the commander of the Snapper.

"Do you claim that the Snapper is a British vessel? "

"Yes, I do! " blustered Captain Flanger recklessly.

"Are you a British subject? "

"No, I am not; but I am not attempting to run the blockade. "

"For what port are you bound? "

"Havana. "

"Have you a clearance for that port? "

"For Havana, and a market. "

"But you have no more idea of going to Havana than you have of going to China, " added the captain of the Chateaugay. "You are bound to Mobile, and you intend to run the blockade; and that intention proved, you are liable to capture. "

"You seem to know my business better than I know it myself, " said Captain Flanger, with a sneer in his tones.

"Perhaps I know it quite as well as you do, at least so far as the voyage of the Snapper is concerned," replied the commander of the Chateaugay, who proceeded to explain international law in relation to the intention to run the blockade. "I shall be able to prove in the court which sits upon your case that you left Nassau for the purpose of running the blockade established at the entrance of Mobile Bay. I presume that will be enough to satisfy both you and the court. In Nassau you did not hesitate to announce your intention to run the blockade, and get into Mobile."

"I should like to see you prove it," growled the captain of the Snapper, in his sneering tones.

"I don't think you would like to see me do it; but I will take you at your word, and prove it now. I have an excellent witness, to whom you made your announcement;" and at this remark Christy stepped out from behind the mainmast, and placed himself in front of the astounded ruffian. "Lieutenant Passford, a naval officer in excellent repute, is all ready to make oath to your assertions."

Captain Flanger and Percy Pierson gazed in silence at the witness, for they supposed he was on the ledge to which he had been transported by the boat. Christy repeated what he had said before, and stated in what manner he had been made a prisoner on board of the Snapper.

"For this outrage in a neutral port I shall hold you and Mr. Pierson as prisoners, leaving the government to determine what steps shall be taken in regard to you; but I trust you will be handed over to the authorities at Nassau, to be properly punished for the outrage."

Of course this decision did not suit Captain Flanger; and Percy Pierson appeared to be intensely alarmed at the prospect before him. Captain Chantor, after consulting with his naval passenger, determined to send the Snapper to Key West, from which she could readily be despatched to New York if occasion should require. Mr. Carlin was appointed prize-master, with a sufficient crew; and at daylight the next morning he sailed for his destination.

The boat which had been sent for the mate and two men belonging to the Snapper put them on board of the steamer; but the captain and the passenger were retained on board of the Chateaugay. The man with the mutilated nose was so disgusted at the loss of his vessel, and with the decision of his captor, that he could not contain himself; and it became necessary not only to restore his irons, but also to commit him to the "brig, " which is the ship's prison.

"What is to become of me, Christy? " asked Percy in the evening, overcome with terror at the prospect before him.

"That is more than I can inform you, " replied Christy coldly.

"But we had no intention of doing you any harm; and we treated you well after you went on board of the Snapper. "

"You committed a dastardly outrage upon me; but your punishment will be left to others. "

"But I had no intention to do you any harm, " pleaded Percy.

"No more lies! You have told me enough since I met you. "

"But I am speaking the truth now, " protested the frightened Southerner.

"No, you are not; the truth is not in you! Did you mean me no harm when you attempted to entice me on board of the Snapper? Did you mean me no harm when you engaged Flanger and his ruffians to make me a prisoner, and put me on board of his steamer? It was a flagrant outrage from beginning to end; for I had the same rights in Nassau that you and your father had, and both of you abused the hospitality of the place when you assaulted me. "

"You were a prisoner of the Confederacy, and had escaped in a blockade-runner; and I thought it was no more than right that you should be returned to your prison, " Percy explained.

"I had the right to escape if I could, and was willing to take the risk; and my capture in Nassau was a cowardly trick. But I did not escape from a Confederate prison. "

"You told me you did. "

"I did not; that was a conclusion to which you jumped with very little help from me. "

Fighting for the Right

"I thought I was doing my duty to my country."

"Then you were an idiot. You have done your best to compromise your country, as you call it, with the British government. If your father is not sent out of Nassau, I shall lose my guess as a Yankee."

"But my father would not allow Captain Flanger to do you any harm; for he was bent upon hanging you as soon as he got out of sight of land, and he sent me with you to see my mother in order to prevent him from carrying out his threat."

"You would have been a powerful preventive in the face of such a brutal ruffian as Captain Flanger," said Christy with a sneer. "You have lied to me before about your father, and I cannot believe anything you say."

"I am speaking the truth now; my father saved your life. I heard him tell Flanger that he would lose the command of the Snapper if any harm came to you."

"If he did so, he did it from the fear of the British authorities. I have nothing more to say about it."

"But as my father saved your life, you ought to stand by me in this scrape," pleaded Percy.

"Whatever was done by you or your father for me, was done from the fear of consequences; and you were the originator of the outrage against me," added Christy, as he descended to the ward room.

The next morning the Snapper was on her voyage to Key West, and the Chateaugay headed for the Hole in the Wall, though she gave it a wide berth, and stood off to the eastward. The next night, being the fourth since the Eleuthera left the ship, the boat containing Mr. Gilfleur was picked up about twenty miles east of the lights. The detective came on board, and was welcomed by the captain, who had been called by his own order.

CHAPTER XXVI

A VISIT TO TAMPA BAY

As soon as Mr. Gilfleur had been welcomed back to the Chateaugay the commander gave the order to the officer of the deck to have the Bahama boat hoisted to the deck, and disposed of as before.

"I beg your pardon, Captain Chantor; but be so kind as to allow the boat to remain alongside, for I must return to Nassau, " interposed the detective.

"Return to Nassau! " exclaimed the captain.

"Yes, sir; it is really necessary that I should do so, for you see that I have come back without Mr. Passford, " replied the Frenchman. "He was attacked by a cowardly ruffian in front of a saloon in the town, and I lost sight of him after that. I have been terribly distressed about him, for the ruffian threatened to kill him, and I fear he has executed his threat. "

"Don't distress yourself for another instant, Mr. Gilfleur, for Mr. Passford is on board of the ship at this moment, and doubtless asleep in his stateroom, " said the captain, cutting short the narrative of the detective.

"On board of the ship! " exclaimed the Frenchman, retreating a few paces in his great surprise. "Impossible! Quite impossible! I found our boat just where we had left it at the back side of the island. "

"But what I say is entirely true; and Mr. Passford wished me to have him called when you came on board, " added the commander, as he sent a quartermaster to summon Christy to the captain's cabin.

"I don't understand how Mr. Passford can be on board of the ship, " continued the bewildered Frenchman. "Ah, he might have hired a boat like the Eleuthera to bring him off. "

"He might have done so, but he did not, " replied Captain Chantor, as he directed the officer of the deck to go ahead, making the course east, as soon as he had secured the detective's boat. "Now, if you will come to my cabin, Mr. Gilfleur, Mr. Passford shall inform you himself that he is on board of the ship; and he has quite an exciting story to tell. "

The commander and the Frenchman went below, and seated themselves in the cabin of the former.

"Mr. Passford has already informed me that the Ovidio is at Nassau, but that she has been seized by a British gunboat for violation of the neutrality laws, " said the captain.

"That is quite true, and it is not probable that the case will be settled for a month to come, " replied Mr. Gilfleur. "But I ascertained by great good luck that her armament was waiting for her at Green Cay, if you know where that is: I do not. "

"It is on the Tongue of the Ocean, as it is called, nearly a hundred miles to the southward of Nassau. I supposed it would be managed in some such way as that, " added the commander. "But do you think it will be a month before her case will be settled? "

"Of course I know nothing about it myself; but I found a court official who was very desirous of talking French, and he invited me to dine with him at his house. I began to ask him questions about the blockade, and the vessels in the harbor; and finally he gave me his opinion that a decision in the case of the Ovidio could not be reached in less than a month, and it might be two mouths. "

At this moment there was a knock at the door of the cabin, and the captain called to the person to come in. Christy, who had taken the time to dress himself fully, opened the door and entered the cabin. The Frenchman leaped from his seat, and embraced the young officer as though he had been his wife or sweetheart, from whom he had been separated for years. Christy, who was not very demonstrative in this direction, submitted to the hugging with the best possible grace, for he knew that the detective was sincere, and had actually grown to love him, perhaps as much for his father's sake as for his own.

"Oh, my dear Mr. Passford, you are to me like one who has come out of his grave, for I have believed for nearly three days that you had been killed by the ruffian that attacked you in the street! " exclaimed Mr. Gilfleur, still pressing both of his late companion's hands in his own. "I was never so rejoiced in all my life, not even when I had unearthed a murderer."

"Perhaps you expected to unearth another murderer," said Christy with a smile.

"That was just what I intended to do. I heard the villanous ruffian swear that he would kill you, and I was almost sure he had done so when you failed to meet me in the rear of the hotel."

At the request of the commander, Christy repeated the story of his adventure in Nassau as briefly as possible, up to the time he had been picked up by the Chateaugay's cutter, and conveyed on board of the ship. The detective was deeply interested, and listened to the narration with the closest attention. At the end of it, he pressed the hand of the young officer again, and warmly congratulated him upon his escape from the enemy.

Mr. Gilfleur then reported more in detail than he had done before, the result of his mission. He gave the names of all the intending blockade-runners in the harbor of Nassau; but the captain declared that he could not capture them on any such evidence as the detective had been able to obtain, for it would not prove the intention.

"The Ovidio may not come out of Nassau for two months to come, and then she will proceed to Green Cay," said Captain Chantor. "I do not think I should be justified in waiting so long for her, especially as she is to run her cargo into Mobile. The blockaders will probably be able to pick her up. I think my mission in the Bahama Islands is finished, and the Chateaugay must proceed to more fruitful fields."

"But you have not made a bad voyage of it so far, Captain Chantor," added Christy. "You sent in the Ionian, sunk the Dornoch, and captured the Cadet and the Snapper, to say nothing of bagging a Confederate commissioner, and the son of another. I should have been glad if you had sent in Colonel Pierson, for he has already done our commerce a great deal of mischief."

"I am entirely satisfied, and doubtless the information obtained here and at the Bermudas will enable our fleet to pick up some more of the steamers you have spotted," added the captain, as he rose from his seat, and dismissed his guests.

Fighting for the Right

The Frenchman was so exhausted by his labors, and the want of sleep, that he retired at once to his room, while Christy went on deck with the commander. The ship had been working to the eastward for over an hour; but the order was given for her to come about, and the course was laid for the light at the Hole in the Wall.

"Now, Mr. Passford, we are bound for the Gulf of Mexico, putting in at Key West for the purpose of attending to the affair of the Snapper," said Captain Chantor. "In a few days more no doubt you will be able to report for duty on board of the Bellevite."

"I shall not be sorry to be on duty again, and especially in the Bellevite," replied Christy, as he went to his stateroom to finish his night's sleep.

The next day the Chateaugay overhauled the Snapper; but all was well on board of her, and the ship proceeded on her course. On the third day she went into the harbor of Key West. Christy and the captain went to work at once on the legal questions relating to the prize last taken. The evidence was deemed sufficient to warrant the sending of her to New York, and on her arrival the prize-master was directed to proceed to that port. Captain Flanger and Percy Pierson were transferred to her, and she sailed the next day; but she encountered a tremendous storm on the Atlantic coast, and was totally wrecked on Hetzel Spit, near Cape Canaveral. The prisoners were put into one boat, which upset, and all in it were drowned, while the other boat, in charge of Lieutenant Carlin, succeeded in reaching the shore of Florida.

The Snapper's case was settled, therefore, outside of the courts. Captain Flanger perished in his wickedness, and Percy Pierson never reached his mother in Mobile. But it was weeks before the news of the disaster reached the Chateaugay and the Bellevite. Christy did not mourn the loss of his great enemy, and he was sorry only that the young man had not lived long enough to become a better man.

The Chateaugay proceeded on her voyage, and reported to the flag-officer of the Eastern Gulf Squadron; by whom she was assigned to a place in the fleet off Appalachicola, while Christy was sent in a tender to the Bellevite, then on duty off the entrance to Mobile Bay.

At this point it became necessary for Christy and Mr. Gilfleur to separate, for the latter was to proceed to New York by a store-ship about to sail. The detective insisted upon hugging him again, and the young officer submitted with better grace than usual to such demonstrations. He had become much attached to his companion in the late enterprises in which they had been engaged, and he respected him very highly for his honesty and earnestness, and admired his skill in his profession. On the voyage from Key West, Christy had written letters to all the members of his family, as well as to Bertha Pembroke, which he committed to the care of Mr. Gilfleur when they parted, not to meet again till the end of the war.

When Christy went on board of the Bellevite he was warmly welcomed by Captain Breaker, who happened to be on deck. Mr. Blowitt was the next to grasp his hand, and before he had done with him, Paul Vapoor, the chief engineer, the young lieutenant's particular crony, hugged him as though he were a brother.

Most of the old officers were still in the ship, and Christy found himself entirely at home where-ever he went on board. He was duly presented to Mr. Walbrook, the third lieutenant, the acting second lieutenant having returned to the flag-ship in the tender.

For all the rest of the year the Bellevite remained on duty as a blockader off Fort Morgan. It was an idle life for the most part, and Christy began to regret that he had caused himself to be transferred from the command of the Bronx. The steamer occasionally had an opportunity to chase a blockade-runner, going in or coming out of the bay. She was the fastest vessel on the station, and she never failed to give a good account of herself.

Late in the year the Bellevite and Bronx were ordered to operate at Tampa Bay, where it was believed that several vessels were loading with cotton. On the arrival of the ships off the bay, a boat expedition was organized to ascertain what vessels were in the vicinity. But the entrance was protected by a battery, and it was supposed that there were field-works in several places on the shores. One of these was discovered just inside of Palm Key, and the Bellevite opened upon it with her big midship gun. Two or three such massive balls were enough for the garrison, and they beat a precipitate retreat, abandoning their pieces. There was water enough to permit the steamer to go into the bay nearly to the town at the head of it.

No other batteries were to be seen, and the Bronx proceeded up the bay, followed by the Bellevite. When the latter had proceeded as far as the depth of water rendered it prudent for her to go at that time of tide, the Bronx went ahead some ten miles farther. The boat expedition, consisting of three cutters from the Bellevite and one from the Bronx, moved towards the head of the bay. Christy, in the second cutter of the Bellevite, was at least two miles from any other boat, when a punt containing a negro put out from the shore near him.

"Are you a frien' ob de colored man?" demanded the negro as soon as he came within speaking-distance of the cutter.

"Within reasonable limits, I am the friend of the colored man," replied Christy, amused at the form of the question.

"What you gwine to do up dis bay, massa?" asked the colored man.

"That will depend upon what we find up this bay."

"You don't 'spect you find no steamers up dis bay, does you, massa?"

"Do you know of any steamers up this bay, my man?" asked Christy. "Do you know of any vessels up here loading with cotton?" asked Christy.

"P'raps I do, massa; and den, again, p'raps I don't know anyt'ing about any vessels," replied the negro, very indefinitely.

Christy was provoked at the manner in which the negro replied to his questions. Ordering his boat's crew to give way with all their might, he directed the cockswain to run for the punt of the negro. The cutter struck it on the broadside, and broke it into two pieces. The boatman was fished up, and hauled on board of the boat.

"The boatman was fished up and hauled on board the boat."

CHAPTER XXVII

AMONG THE KEYS OF TAMPA

Christy Passford did not intend to cut the negro's punt into two pieces, though perhaps there was some mischief in the purpose of the cockswain. The boatman gave him an evasive answer to his question, which provoked the young officer. The punt was a very old affair, reduced almost to punk by the decay of the boards of which it was built, or the bow of the cutter would not have gone through it so readily. The lieutenant had simply desired to get alongside the negro's shaky craft in order to question him, for he was satisfied from the fellow's manner that he knew more than he pretended to know.

The boatman had come off from the shore of his own accord; he had not been solicited to give any information, and his movements had been entirely voluntary on his own part. Yet Christy was sorry that his punt had been stove, valueless as the craft had been; for, as a rule, the colored people were friendly to the Union soldiers, and he was not disposed to do them any injury.

As soon as the officer in charge of the boat saw that the bow was likely to strike the punt, he directed the cockswain to stop and back her, which was done, but too late to save the flimsy box from destruction. The two bowmen drew in the negro without any difficulty; and so expeditiously had he been rescued that he was not wet above the hips. He had been caught up just as the bow of the cutter cut into the punt.

"That was well done, bowmen, " said Christy, as the boatman was placed upon his feet in the fore sheets.

The negro was rather small in stature, and black enough to save all doubts in regard to his parentage; but there was an expression of cunning in his face not often noticed in persons of his race. The coast of Florida, south of the entrance to Tampa Bay, as in many other portions, is fringed with keys, or cays as they are called in the West Indies, which are small islands, though many of them are ten miles in length. This fringe of keys extended up Tampa Bay for over twenty miles; and it was from behind one of them that the punt had put out when Christy's boat approached. The negro had been obliged to paddle at least half a mile to come within speaking-distance of the cutter.

"You done broke my boat in two pieces!" exclaimed the boatman, gazing at the two parts of the floating wreck. "Don't t'ink you is a frien' ob de colored man widin no limits at all, or you don't smash his boat like dat."

"That was an accident, my friend," replied Christy. "How much was the punt worth?"

"Dat boat wan't no punk, massa, and it was wuf two dollars in good money," replied the colored man, his eyes brightening, and his expression of cunning becoming more intense, when he realized the possibility of being paid for his loss.

"If you give me the information I desire, I will pay for the boat," added Christy, who proposed to do so out of his own pocket, for his father was a millionaire of several degrees, and the son had very nearly made a fortune out of the prizes, from which he had received an officer's share.

"Tank you, massa; I'm a poor man, and I git my livin' gwine fishin' in dat boat you done stove."

"What is your name, my man?"

"Quimp, sar; and dat's de short for Quimple," replied the colored person of this name.

"Where do you live?"

"Ober on de shor dar, in de woods."

"How deep is the water inside of these keys, Quimp?" asked Christy, pointing to the long, narrow islands which lined the south-easterly side of the bay.

"Not much water inside dem keys dar, sar," replied the boatman, looking off in the other direction.

"But there are deep places in there, I am very sure."

"Yes, sar; ten feet in some places, " replied Quimp, suddenly becoming more communicative. "When de wind blow from de west or de norf-west, dar's twelve foot inside de long key. "

"Do you know of any vessels, any schooners, or steamers, inside the bay, Quimp? " asked Christy, pushing his inquiries a point farther.

"Couldn't told you, massa, " replied the boatman, shaking his head.

"Do you mean that you don't know, my man? "

"Dis nigger done got but one head, and it's wuf more to him dan it is to any oder feller, massa; and it don't do for him to tell no stories about vessels and steamers, " replied Quimp, shaking his head more vigorously.

"I suppose you have a family, Quimp? "

"No, sar; done got no family. De ole woman done gone to glory more'n ten years ago, and de boys done growed up and gone off. No, sar; dis nigger got no family. "

"Then you don't care to stay here, where you have to work hard for little money? " suggested Christy.

"Money! Don't see no money. Nobody but white folks got any money; and dey has next to noffin in dese times. "

"I will pay you well for any information that may be of importance to me, and I will take you on board of a man-of-war farther down the bay, if you are afraid of losing your head. "

"If dis nigger told some stories he lose his head for sartin, " added Quimp, shaking his head, as if to make sure that it safely rested on his shoulders.

"If you tell me the truth, you shall be protected. "

"Wot you want to know, massa? " demanded Quimp, as though he was weakening in his resolution.

Christy could not help wondering why the boatman had come out from behind the key, if he was not willing to impart his knowledge to the officer of the boat, for he could not help understanding the object of the gunboats in visiting the bay; and the Bellevite lay not half a mile below the northern end of what Quimp called the long key.

"I want to know if there are any steamers or other vessels in the bay," replied Christy, coming directly to the point. "If there are any, we shall find them; but you can save us the trouble of looking for them."

"How much you gwine to gib me, massa, if I told you?" asked the negro, as he walked between the men on the thwarts to the stern sheets, in order to be nearer to the officer.

"I will give you ten dollars if you will be sure and tell me the truth."

"Dis nigger don't never told no lies, massa," protested Quimp. "If you pay me five dollars for de boat you done stove, and"—

"But you said the boat was worth only two dollars," interposed the officer.

"Dat's de gospel truf, massa; but it costs me five dollars to get a new boat, to say noffin about de time. I mought starve to def afore I can get a boat."

The negro's argument was logical, and Christy admitted its force, and expressed his willingness to pay the price demanded.

"Five dollars for de boat, massa, and ten dollars for tellin' de whole truf," added Quimp.

"All right, my man," added the lieutenant.

"Yes, sar; but I want de money now, sar," said Quimp, extending his hand to receive it; and Christy thought he was very sharp for one in his position.

"I will pay you when you have imparted the information," he replied; and, for some reason he could not explain, he was not satisfied with the conduct of the negro.

He was altogether too shrewd for one who appeared to be so stupid. The expression of cunning in his face told against him, and perhaps it was this more than anything else that prejudiced the officer. He took it for granted that he should have to take the boatman off to the Bellevite with him, and that it would be time enough to pay him on board of the ship.

"Dat won't do, massa! " protested Quimp earnestly. "What you tink? Suppose dar is a steamer in de bay loaded wid cotton, all ready to quit for somewhar. Do you tink, massa, I can go on bord of her wid you? No, sar! Dis nigger lose his head for sartin if dem uns knows I pilot you to dat steamer. You done got two eyes, massa, and you can see it for shore. "

"But I can protect you, Quimp, " suggested Christy.

"No, sar! All de sojers in de Yankee camp could not save me, sar. De first man dat sees me will knive me in de heart, or cut my froat from one ear to de oder! " protested Quimp more earnestly than before, though he manifested no terror in his words or manner.

"Very well, Quimp; I will pay you the money as soon as we see the steamer or other vessel, and then assist you to make your escape, " replied Christy. "I will go a step farther, and pay you for the boat now; but I will not pay you the ten dollars till you show us a vessel. "

While the negro was scratching his head to stimulate his ideas, the officer handed him a gold sovereign and a shilling of English money, provided for his visit to Bermuda and Nassau, which made a little more than five dollars.

"I don't reckon a gemman like you would cheat a poor nigger, " said Quimp, while his eyes were still glowing with delight at the sight of the money in his hand.

"Certainly not, my man, " replied Christy, laughing at the idea. "Just as soon as I get my eye on the steamer of which you speak, I will pay you the ten dollars in gold and silver. "

"I don't know much about dis yere money, massa, " said the boatman, still studying the coin.

Fighting for the Right

"The gold piece is an English sovereign, worth about four dollars and eighty-five cents; and the silver coin is a shilling, worth very nearly a quarter of a dollar; so that I have paid you over five dollars."

"Yes, sar, tank you, sar. Cap'n Stopfoot fotched over some ob de money like dat from Nassau, and I done seen it."

"But I can't stop to talk all day, Quimp," continued Christy impatiently. "If you are going to do anything to earn your ten dollars, it is time for you to be about it."

"Yes, sar; I will told you all about it, massa."

"No long yarns, my man!" protested the officer, as Quimp seated himself in the stern sheets as though he intended to tell a long story.

"Yes, massa; told you all about it in a bref. De wind done blow fresh from de norf-west for t'ree days; dat's what Massa Cap'n Stopfoot say," Quimp began.

"No matter what Captain Stopfoot says!" Christy interposed. "Tell me where the steamer is, if there is any steamer in the bay. We will stop the foot and the mouth of Captain Stopfoot when we come to him."

"Well, sar, if you don't want to har dis nigger's yarn, he'll shet up all to onct," replied Quimp, standing on his dignity.

"Go on, then; but make it short," added Christy, finding it would take less time to get what he wanted out of the negro by letting him have his own way. "Wind fresh from the north-west for three days."

"Yes, sar; and dat pile up de water so de tide rise six or eight inches higher," continued Quimp, picking up the clew given him. "High tide in one hour from now, and de Reindeer was gwine out den for shore. Dat's de whole story, massa, and not bery long."

"All right, Quimp. Now where is the Reindeer?"

"Ober de oder side ob long key, massa. Dar's more'n four fadoms ob water under dis boat now, and twelve feet 'tween de two keys," added the boatman, whose tongue was fully unlocked by this time.

Fighting for the Right

The crew of the cutter were directed to give way, and the negro pointed out the channel which led inside the keys.

CHAPTER XXVIII

THE SURRENDER OF THE REINDEER

Christy looked over the side of the boat, and saw that the water was quite clear. The channel, which lay in the middle of the bay, had four and a quarter fathoms of water at mean low tide, according to the chart the officer had with him. He had brought several copies of the large chart with him from New York, and he had cut them up into convenient squares, so that they could be easily handled when he was on boat service. But his authority gave no depth of water on the shoal sands.

In a short time the boat came to the verge of the channel, and Christy directed the bowman to stand by with the lead, with which the boat was provided. The first heaving gave three and a half fathoms, and it gradually decreased at each report, till only two fathoms and a quarter was indicated, when the boat was between the two keys, the southern of which Quimp called the long key, simply because that was the longest in the bay, and not because it was a proper name.

"Now, Massa Ossifer, look sharp ober on de starboard side, " said the negro.

"I don't see anything, " replied Christy.

"No, sar, not yet; but look ober dat way, and you see somet'ing fo' yore t'ree minutes older, massa. "

Christy fixed his gaze on the point of the long key, beyond which Quimp intimated that the steamer would be seen.

"Now, Massa Ossifer, fo' yore two minutes nearer glory, you'll see de end ob de bowsprit ob de Reindeer, " added Quimp, who was beginning to be somewhat excited, possibly in expectation of receiving his ten dollars; and perhaps he was regretting that he had not demanded twenty.

"How big is that steamer, Quimp? " asked the officer of the cutter.

"Fo' hund'ed tons, massa; dat's what Cap'n Stopfoot done say, kase I never done measure her. He done say she is very flat on her bottom, and don't draw much water for her size, " replied the negro. "Dar's de end ob de bowsprit, massa! " he exclaimed at this moment.

"Way enough, cockswain! " said Christy sharply. "Stern all! "

The headway of the cutter was promptly checked, and she was set back a couple of lengths, when the order was given to the crew to lay on their oars.

"W'at's the matter, Massa Ossifer? Arn't you gwine no furder? " asked Quimp.

"I have seen enough of the Reindeer to satisfy me that she is there; and I have stopped the boat to give you a chance to make your escape, " replied Christy. "I don't want you to lose your head for the service you have rendered to me. "

"Dis nigger can't get away from here, massa, " replied the boatman, looking about him. "A feller can't swim a mile when de water's full ob alligators. Dem varmints like niggers to eat jus' as well as dey do white men. "

Christy had his doubts about there being alligators of a dangerous size in the bay, though he had seen small ones in other bays of the coast; but he was willing to admit that Quimp knew better about the matter than he did. It was a hard swim to any other key than the long one, to which the cutter was quite near. He could land the negro on that key, but he would reveal the presence of the boat to the people on board of the Reindeer, and they would burn her rather than have her fall into the hands of the Union navy.

"I can land you on the long key, Quimp, " suggested the officer.

"No, sar! Can't go there; for Cap'n Stopfoot sartainly cotch me dar, " protested the negro.

"I don't think so, Quimp. "

"De ossifers and men ob de Reindeer will go asho' when you done took de steamer; don't you see dat, massa? "

"What shall I do with you then? " asked Christy, as he handed him two sovereigns and two shillings.

"T'ank you, sar; dat's a pile ob money! " exclaimed Quimp, as he looked with admiration upon the coins.

"It is what I agreed to give you. But what shall I do with you now? That is the question I want answered, " continued the officer impatiently.

"You can't do not'ing wid me, Massa Ossifer, and I must tooken my chance to go up in de boat. Better hab my froat cut 'n be chawed up by a big alligator. Was you ever bit by an alligator, Massa Ossifer? "

"I never was. "

"I knows about dat, massa, " added Quimp, as he bared his leg, and showed an ugly scar.

Christy would not wait to hear any more, but ordered the cockswain to go ahead again. It looked to him that Quimp, now that he had received his money, and made fifteen dollars out of his morning's work, was intentionally delaying the object of the expedition, for what reason he could form no clear idea.

"I spose, if Captain Stopfoot kill me for w'at I done do, you'll bury me side de old woman dat done gone to glory ten year ago? " continued the negro, who did not look old enough to have buried a wife ten years before.

"I am not in the burying business, my friend, and after you are dead, you had better send for your sons to do the job, for they will know where to find the grave of the departed companion of your joys and sorrows, " replied Christy, as the boat came in sight of the bowsprit of the Reindeer again.

"My sons done gone away to Alabamy, sar, and" —

"That's enough about that. There are no alligators about here, and you can swim ashore if you are so disposed; but you must shut up your wide mouth and keep still if you stay in the boat. Heave the lead, bowman! "

"Mark under water two, sir, " reported the leadsman.

Fighting for the Right

In a few moments more the cutter had gained a position where the steamer could be fully seen. She was a side-wheeler, and appeared to be a very handsome vessel. She had a considerable deck-load of cotton, and doubtless her hold was filled with the same valuable commodity.

"Is that steamer armed, Quimp? " asked Christy, who could see no signs of life on board of her.

"She don't got no arms, but she hab two field-pieces on her for'ad deck, " replied the negro.

"How many men has she on board? "

"L'em me see: the cap'n and de mate is two, two ingineers, two firemen; dat makes six; and den she hab two deck-hands. "

"But that makes only eight in all, " replied Christy. "Are you sure that is all? "

"Dead shoar dat's all, Massa Ossifer. "

"But that is not enough to handle the steamer on a voyage to a foreign port, for I dare say she is going to Nassau, " added Christy, who was on the lookout for some piece of strategy by which his boat and its crew might be destroyed.

"I don't know not'ing about dat, sar; but Cap'n Stopfoot is a pow'ful smart man; and he's Yankee too. I done hear him say he gwine to j'in de Yankee navy. "

What Quimp said was rather suspicious; but Christy could see nothing to justify his doubts. He directed the cockswain to steer the cutter as closely to the side of the Reindeer as the movement of the oars would permit, so that the field-pieces could not be brought to bear upon it. The steamer lay at a sort of temporary pier, which had evidently been erected for her accommodation, and the cotton had doubtless been brought to the key by river steamers by the Suwanee and other streams from cotton regions.

There was no habitation or other building on the shore, but a gangway was stretched to the land, over which a couple of men were hastening on board when the cutter reached the stern of the

Reindeer. From appearances Christy judged that the water had been deepened by dredges, for a considerable quantity of sand and mud was disposed in heaps in the shallow water a hundred feet or more from the rude wharf.

"Boat ahoy! " shouted a person on board, near the starboard accommodation ladder, which the officer of the boat had noticed was in place.

"On board the steamer! " replied Christy.

"What is your business here? " inquired the person on the deck of the Reindeer, though he could not be seen from the cutter.

"I will go on board and inform you, " replied Christy.

As there were no signs of resistance on board of the vessel, the officer of the cutter directed his men to make a dash for the accommodation ladder, which had the appearance of having been left to make things convenient for a boarding-party. The crew were all armed with a cutlass and revolver in the belt.

"Lay her aboard! " said Christy, quietly enough, as he led the way himself, for he was a bold leader, and was not content to follow his men. As he leaped down from the bulwarks to the deck, he confronted the person who had hailed him in the boat.

"What is your business on board of the Reindeer? " demanded, in a very tame tone, the man in front of him.

"I am an officer of the United States navy, and my business is to make a prize of this steamer and her cargo, " replied Christy.

"Is that so? You did not give me your name, sir, " added the man.

"Lieutenant Passford, attached to the United States steamer Bellevite. Do me the favor to explain who you are, sir, " returned Christy.

"I am Captain Solomon Stopfoot, in command of the Reindeer, at your service, born and brought up on Long Island, " answered the commander of the steamer.

Fighting for the Right

"Then what are you doing here?" demanded the naval officer. "Where were you born on Long Island?"

"In Babylon, on the south shore."

"Then Babylon is fallen!" exclaimed Christy, indignant to find a man born so near his own home doing the dirty work of the Confederate government.

"Perhaps not; and perhaps you may change your view of me when you have heard my story," added Captain Stopfoot.

"Well, Captain, there is only one story that I care to hear just now, and its title is simply 'Surrender,'" replied Christy rather impatiently. "You understand my business on board of the Reindeer; and if you propose to make any resistance, it is time for you to begin."

"It would be folly for me to make any resistance, and I shall not make any. I have only two engineers, two firemen, foreigners, hired in Nassau, who would not fight if I wished them to do so, and two deck-hands. I could do nothing against the eight well-armed men you have brought on board. I surrender."

"I should say that was a wise step on your part, Captain Stopfoot," replied Christy. "When you are more at leisure, I hope you will indulge me in an explanation of the manner in which a Long Islander happens to be engaged in blockade-running."

"I am an American citizen now, as I have always been; I shall be only too happy to get back under the old flag. As an evidence of my sincerity, I will assist you in getting the Reindeer out of this place. The tide is high at this moment; and half an hour from now it will be too late to move the vessel," said Captain Stopfoot, with every appearance of sincerity in his manner.

"I will see you, Captain, as soon as I have looked the steamer over," replied Christy, as he left the commander of the Reindeer at the door of his cabin, and went forward to examine the vessel.

He found the steam up; and the engineer bowed to him as he looked into his room. There was nothing to be seen but cotton, piled high on the deck, and stuffed into the hold; and he returned to the cabin.

CHAPTER XXIX

BRINGING OUT THE PRIZE

It seemed to Christy, after he had completed his examination of the Reindeer, that she carried an enormous deck-load for a steamer of her size, and that the bales were piled altogether too high for a vessel that was liable to encounter a heavy sea. But the cotton was where it could be readily thrown overboard if the safety of the steamer was threatened by its presence. He found only the six men mentioned by Stopfoot, though he had looked in every part of the vessel, even to the fire-room and the quarters of the crew and firemen.

"I find everything as you stated, Captain Stopfoot; but I should say that you were proposing to go to sea short-handed. I did not even see a person whom I took for the mate. Is it possible that you could get along without one? " said Christy, when he met the commander at the door of the cabin.

"The truth is, that my men deserted me when they saw the two men-of-war come into the bay, for they knew I had no adequate means of making a defence. In fact, the Reindeer was as good as captured as soon as your two steamers came into the bay, for you were morally sure to find her, " replied the captain.

"But where are your men? How could they get away? " asked Christy.

"They have not got away a great distance. You could see the gangway to the shore; and all they had to do was to land, without even the trouble of taking to a boat. They are all on the long key; and without some sort of a craft they will not be able to leave it. If you desire to spend your time in hunting them down, I have no doubt you could find them all. "

"How many of them are there on the island, Captain Stopfoot? "

"The mate, four deck-hands, and two firemen. It would not be a difficult task for you to capture them all, for I did not look upon them as fighting material; they have crowded about all the men of that sort into the army. "

"I have no desire to find them, and they may stay on the key till doomsday, so far as I am concerned, " replied Christy. "We don't regard the men employed on blockade-runners as of much account. But it is time to get under way, Captain; I have men enough to do all the work, and I think I have learned the channel well enough to find the way out into the deep water of the bay. "

"As I said before, Lieutenant Passford, I am willing to assist you, for I am anxious to get back among my own people, and to find a position in the old navy. I have been master of a vessel for the last ten years, and I know the Southern coast better than most of your officers. "

"No doubt you will find a place when you want one, for all competent men are taken, " replied Christy, as he went to the quarter to see if the Bellevite's cutter was in condition to be towed by the Reindeer.

He had left the boat in charge of Quimp, or rather he had left him in it without assigning any particular duty to him. He was no longer in the cutter, and the officer concluded that he had taken to the long key, and was fraternizing with the renegades who had deserted the Reindeer. The long painter of the boat was taken to the stern and made fast in a suitable place, and Christy hastened to the forward part of the vessel with six of his men, leaving a quartermaster, who was the cockswain of the cutter, with two others, in charge of the after part.

On his way he went into the engine-room, which opened from the main deck, where he had before seen the two engineers, the chief of whom had received him very politely. He suggested to the captain that he had made no arrangement with these officers, and he was not quite sure that they would be willing to do duty now that the steamer was a prize.

"There will be no trouble about them, for they are Englishmen, engaged at Nassau, and they will do duty as long as they are paid for it, as they have no interest in the quarrel between the North and the South, " said Captain Stopfoot; and Christy could not help seeing that he was making everything very comfortable for him.

"We are willing to work for whoever will pay us, " added the chief engineer, "and without asking any hard questions. "

"I will see that you are paid, " returned Christy. "You will attend to the bells as usual, will you? "

"Yes, sir; we will do our duty faithfully, " answered the chief.

Christy and the captain proceeded to the pilot-house, which appeared to have been recently added to the vessel to suit the taste of her American owners. The naval officer stationed one of his own men at the wheel, and then took a careful survey of the position of the steamer. He directed his crew to cast off the fasts.

"Is there a United States flag on board of this craft, Captain Stopfoot?" asked Christy.

"To be sure there is, Lieutenant, " said the captain with a laugh; "but I do not get much chance to get under its folds. "

"Of course you have Confederate flags in abundance? "

"Enough of them, " replied the commander, as he drew forth from a signal-box the flags required. "What do you intend to do with these?"

"I intend to hoist the United States flag over the Confederate to show that this steamer is a prize, otherwise the Bellevite might put a shot through her as soon as she shows herself outside of the key, " replied Christy.

"A wise precaution, " added Captain Stopfoot.

The naval officer rang one bell as one of his men reported to him that the fasts had been cast off, and that all was clear. The grating sound of the engine was immediately heard, with the splash of the paddle wheels. Very slowly the Reindeer began to move forward. Christy had very carefully noted the bearings of the channel by which the steamer must pass out into the deep water of the bay, and the instructions which the captain volunteered to give him were not necessary.

"I suppose I am as really a Northern man in principle as you are, Mr. Passford, " said the captain, as the steamer crept very cautiously through the pass between the keys.

"If you are, you have taken a different way to show it, " replied Christy, glancing at the speaker.

"But the circumstances have compelled me to remain in the service of my Southern employer until the present time, and this promises to be the first favorable opportunity to escape from it that has been presented to me, " Captain Stopfoot explained.

"You have been to Nassau a number of times, I judge; and it was possible for you to abandon your employment any time you pleased," suggested the naval officer.

"It was not so easy a matter as you seem to think; for there were no Northern vessels there in which I could take passage to New York, or any other loyal port.

"Mr. Groomer, the mate of the Reindeer, is part owner of her, though he is not competent to navigate a vessel at sea, and he kept close watch of me all the time, on shore as well as on board. "

"But I understand that Mr. Groomer, the mate, has deserted you, and gone on shore with the others of your ship's company, " added Christy, rather perplexed at the situation indicated by the captain.

"What else could he do? "

"What else could you do? and why did you not abandon the steamer when he did so? If one of the owners would not stand by the vessel, why did you do so? "

"I have told you before why I did not: because I wish to get back to my friends in the North, and find a place in the old navy, which would be more congenial to me than selling cotton for the benefit of the Confederacy, " replied Captain Stopfoot with considerable energy.

The explanation seemed to be a reasonable one, and Christy could not gainsay it, though he was not entirely satisfied with the declarations of the commander. He admitted that he regarded the Reindeer as good as captured when he saw the Bellevite and Bronx come into the bay; and he could easily have escaped in a boat to one of the gunboats after the watchful mate "took to the woods, " as he had literally done, for the key was partly covered with small trees.

"And a quarter two!" reported the leadsman who had been stationed on the forecastle.

"The water don't seem to vary here," added Christy.

"No, for the owners had done some dredging in this channel; in fact, there was hardly anything like a channel here when they began the work," replied Captain Stopfoot. "To which of the steamers do you belong, Mr. Passford?"

"To the Bellevite, the one which lies below the long key. The other has gone up the bay."

"She has gone on a fruitless errand, for there is not another vessel loading in these waters," said the captain. "I suppose you will report on board of the Bellevite, Mr. Passford?"

"Of course I shall not leave the Reindeer without an order from the commander of the ship," replied the lieutenant.

"And a half two!" shouted the leadsman.

"The channel deepens," said Christy.

"You will be in deep water in five minutes."

On this report Christy rang four bells, and the Reindeer went ahead at full speed.

"By the mark three!" called the man at the lead.

The water was deepening rapidly, and presently the report of three and a half fathoms came from the forecastle. It was soon followed by "And a half four," upon which the lieutenant directed the wheelman to steer directly for the Bellevite. He had hardly given the order before the report of heavy firing from the upper waters of the bay came to his ear.

"What can that be?" he asked, looking at Captain Stopfoot.

"I don't know; but I suppose that the gunboat which went up the bay is firing at some battery she has discovered. They have strengthened the works in that direction which defend the town, since the only one there was silenced by one of your gunboats, " the captain explained.

The guns were heard on board of the Bellevite, and she began to move up the bay as though she intended to proceed to the assistance of her consort. Mr. Blowitt in the first cutter had followed the Bronx, and the third cutter, in charge of Mr. Lobscott, had gone over to Piney Point, to which there was a channel with from three to five fathoms of water, and which seemed to be a favorable place to load a vessel with cotton.

As the Reindeer approached the Bellevite, the latter stopped her screw, and Christy directed the wheelman to run the steamer alongside, and within twenty or thirty feet of her. There was no sea in the bay, and there was no danger in doing so. As the Reindeer approached the position indicated, two bells were struck to stop her. The flags that had been hoisted on board, informed Captain Breaker of the capture of the steamer, so that no report was necessary.

"I have to report the capture of the Reindeer, loaded with cotton, and ready to sail for Nassau, " said Christy, mounting one of the high piles of cotton bales, and saluting the commander of the Bellevite, who had taken his place on the rail to see the prize.

"Do you know the cause of the firing up the bay, Mr. Passford? " asked Captain Breaker.

"I do not, Captain; but I learn that the battery below the town has been strengthened, and I should judge that the Bronx had engaged it."

"Have you men enough to hold your prize, Mr. Passford? "

"I think I have, Captain. "

"You will go down the bay, and anchor outside of Egmont Key. "

Christy rang one bell, and then four.

CHAPTER XXX

A VERY IMPORTANT SERVICE

The Reindeer went ahead at full speed, while the Bellevite stood up the bay, picking up the crew of Mr. Blowitt's boat on the way, evidently with the intention of taking part in the action which the Bronx had initiated. The loud reports at intervals indicated that the Bronx was using her big midship gun, while the feebler sounds proved that the metal of the battery was much lighter. The prize was not a fast steamer, and she was over an hour in making the dozen miles to Egmont Island, on which was the tower of a lighthouse forty feet high, but no use was made of it at that time.

The Bellevite proceeded very slowly, sounding all the time; but at the end of half an hour the Reindeer was at least ten miles from her, which was practically out of sight and hearing. About this time Christy observed that Captain Stopfoot left the pilot-house, where he had remained from the first; but he paid no attention to him. He had three men on the quarter-deck of the steamer, one in the pilot-house with him, and five more in other parts of the vessel.

Christy knew the channel to the south of the lighthouse, and piloted the steamer to a point about half a mile to the westward of the island. He was looking through one of the forward windows of the pilot-house, selecting a proper place to come to anchor, in accordance with the orders of Captain Breaker. While he was so engaged he heard some sort of a disturbance in the after part of the steamer.

"On deck there! " he called sharply; and the five men who had been stationed in this part of the steamer stood up before him, jumping up from the beds they had made for themselves on the cotton bales, or rushing out from behind them. "Hopkins and White, go aft and ascertain the cause of that disturbance, " he added.

The two men promptly obeyed the order, and the naval officer directed the other three to stand by to anchor the steamer. In a few minutes the anchor was ready to let go. Perhaps a quarter of an hour had elapsed, when Christy began to wonder what had become of the two men he had sent aft to report on the disturbance.

"Linman," he called to one of the three men on the forecastle, "go aft and see what has become of Hopkins and White."

Linman proceeded to obey the order, but had not been gone twenty seconds, before the noise of another disturbance came to Christy's ears, and this time it sounded very much like a scuffle. Up to this moment, and even since Captain Stopfoot had left the pilot-house, Christy had not suspected that anything on board was wrong. The sounds that came from the after part of the vessel excited his suspicions, though they did not assure him that the ship's company of the steamer were engaged in anything like a revolt.

"Follow me, Bench and Kingman!" he shouted to the two men that remained on the forecastle. "Strike two bells, Landers," he added to the wheelman.

Christy had drawn the cutlass he carried in his belt, and was ready, with the assistance of the two men he had called, to put down any insubordination that might have been manifested by the ship's company of the prize. He would have been willing to admit, if he had given the matter any attention at that moment, that it was the natural right of the captured captain and his men to regain possession of their persons and property by force and violence; but he was determined to make it dangerous for them to do so.

"On the forecastle, sir!" exclaimed Landers, the wheelman.

Christy had put his hand upon the door of the pilot-house to open it as the two men were moving aft; but he looked out the window at the exclamation of the wheelman. The cotton bales seemed to have become alive all at once, for half a dozen of them rolled over like a spaniel just out of the water, and four men leaped out from under them, or from apertures which had been formed beneath them.."

Bench and Kingman seemed to be bewildered, and both of them were thrown down by the movement of the bales. The four men who had so suddenly appeared sprang upon them, and almost in the twinkling of an eye had tied their hands behind them. Christy drew one of the revolvers from his belt; but he did not fire, for he was as likely to hit his own men as their assailants. The victors in the struggle dragged the two men into the forecastle, and disappeared themselves.

Fighting for the Right

Christy was almost confounded by the suddenness of the attack; but he did not give up the battle, for he had at least six men in the after part of the steamer. Bidding Landers draw his cutlass and follow him, he rushed out at the door he had before opened. He could not see anything aft but the walls of cotton bales, with a narrow passage between them and the bulwarks. He moved aft with his eyes wide open; but he had not gone ten feet before a man dropped down upon him from the top of the deck-load with so much force as to carry him down to the planks.

"His assailant put his arms around him and hugged him like a bear."

His assailant put his arms around him and hugged him like a bear, so that he could neither use his cutlass nor his revolvers. At the same moment another man dropped down on Landers in like manner. It was impossible to resist an attack made from overhead, where it was least expected, and when they were taken by surprise. Christy was a prisoner, and his hands were bound behind him.

At this moment Captain Stopfoot presented himself before the prize-master, his face covered with smiles, and nervous from the excess of his joy at the recapture of the Reindeer. Christy could not see what had become of the rest of his men. He knew that three of them had been secured, but he did not know what had become of the other six, and he had some hope that they had escaped their assailants, and were in condition to render him needed assistance, for it seemed impossible that all of them could have been overcome.

In spite of his chagrin and mortification, Christy could not help seeing that the affair on the part of Captain Stopfoot had been well managed, and that the author of the plot was smart enough to be a Yankee, whether he was one or not. It was evident enough now that the mate and the rest of the crew had not "taken to the woods, " but had been concealed in such dens as could be easily made among the cotton bales.

"I hope you are not very uncomfortable, Mr. Passford, " said Captain Stopfoot, as he presented his smiling face before his late captor.

"Physically, I am not very uncomfortable, in spite of these bonds; but otherwise, I must say that I am. I am willing to acknowledge that it is a bad scrape for me, " replied Christy as good-naturedly as possible, for his pride would not allow him to let the enemy triumph over him.

"That would not be at all unnatural, and I think it is a very bad scrape for a naval officer of your high reputation to get into, " added the captain. "But I desire to say, Mr. Passford, that I have no ill-will towards you, and it will not be convenient for me to send you to a Confederate prison, important as such a service would be to our cause. "

"I judge that you are not as anxious as you were to get into the old navy, " added Christy.

"I confess that I am not, and that I should very much prefer to obtain a good position in the Confederate navy. I hope you will excuse the little fictions in which I indulged for your amusement. I was born in the very heart of the State of Alabama, and never saw Long Island in all my life, " continued the captain. "By the way, my mate is not part owner of the Reindeer, though he is just as faithful to her interests as though he owned the whole of her; and it was he that pounced down upon you at the right moment. I assure you he is a very good fellow, and I hope you will not have any grudge against him. "

"Not the least in the world, Captain Stopfoot, " replied Christy.

"I hope I shall not be obliged to detain you long, Mr. Passford; and I shall not unless one of your gunboats chases me. I shall endeavor to put you and your men on shore at the Gasparilla Pass, where you can hail one of the gunboats as it comes along in pursuit of the Reindeer, though I hope they will not sail for this purpose before night. "

"The Bellevite is not likely to discover the absence of the prize at present, for she will have to remain up the bay over one tide, " said the mate.

"That is what I was calculating upon, " added the captain. "Now, Mr. Passford, I shall be compelled to take my leave of you, for we have to stow the cotton over again before we go to sea. I am exceedingly obliged to you for the very valuable service you have rendered me. "

"I was not aware that I had rendered you any service, " replied Christy, wondering what he could mean.

"You are not? Then your perception is not as clear as I supposed it was. When it was reported to me that two gunboats were coming into the bay I considered the Reindeer as good as captured, as I have hinted to you before. My cargo will bring a fortune in Nassau, and I am half owner of the steamer and her cargo, if Mr. Groomer, the mate, is not. I was almost in despair, for I could not afford to lose my vessel and her valuable cargo. I considered myself utterly ruined. But just then I got an idea, and I came to a prompt decision; " and the captain paused.

"And what was that decision? " asked Christy curiously.

"When I saw your boat coming, for I was on the long key, I determined that you should bring the Reindeer out into the Gulf, and save me all trouble and anxiety in regard to her, and I knew that you could do it a great deal better than I could. Wherefore I am extremely grateful to you for this very important service, " said Captain Stopfoot, bowing very politely. "But I am compelled to leave you now to your own pleasant reflections. Mr. Passford, I shall ask you and your men to take possession of the cabin, and not show yourselves on deck; and you will pardon me if I lock the door upon you. "

The captive officer followed the captain aft to the door of the cabin. On a bale of cotton he saw the cutlasses and revolvers which had been taken from him and his men, which had apparently been thrown in a heap where they happened to hit, and had been forgotten. Seated on the cotton he found all his men, with their hands tied behind them. Captain Stopfoot opened the cabin door, and directed his prisoners to enter.

"Excuse me for leaving you so abruptly, Mr. Passford, " continued the captain while he was feeling in his pocket for the key of the door. "It looks as though it were going to blow before night, and I must get ready for it. Besides, the Bellevite may return on the present tide, and I am informed that she is a very fast sailer, as the Reindeer is not, and I must make the most of my opportunity; but when my fortune is made out of my present cargo, I shall owe it largely to you. Adieu for the present. "

Captain Stopfoot left the cabin, locking the door behind him. The hands of the prisoners, ten in number, were tied behind them with ropes, for probably the steamer was not provided with handcuffs. Christy examined his men in regard to the manner in which they had been overcome. The three men who had been left near the cabin door had been overthrown by those who jumped down upon them when they were separated, one at the stern, one on the bales, watching the Bellevite in the distance, and the third asleep on a cotton bale. The lieutenant had seen the rest of the enterprise.

"This thing is not going to last long, my men, " said Christy, who realized that he should never be able to stand up under the obloquy of having brought out a blockade-runner for the enemy.

He caused the hands to march in front of him till he found one who had been carelessly bound. He backed this one up in the rear of Calwood, the quartermaster, and made him untie the line, which he could do with his fingers, though his wrists were bound. It was not the work of three minutes to unbind the rest of them.

Christy broke a pane of glass in the door, and unlocked it with the key the captain had left in the keyhole.

CHAPTER XXXI

AN UNDESIRED PROMOTION

As Christy unlocked the cabin door, he discovered a negro lying on the deck, as close as he could get to the threshold. The man attempted to spring to his feet, but the officer seized him by the hair of the head, and pulled him into the cabin.

"Here, Calwood, put your hand over this fellow's mouth!" said Christy to the quartermaster, who laid violent hands on him, assisted by Norlock.

The latter produced a handkerchief, which he thrust into the mouth of the negro, so that he could not give the alarm. All the men were alert and eager to wipe out the shame, as they regarded it, of the disaster; and those who had been stationed near the cabin had certainly been wanting in vigilance. Two of them seized a couple of the lines with which they had been bound, and tied the arms of the negro behind him.

A second look at the negro assured Christy that it was Quimp, and he was more mortified than before at the trick which had been played upon him. Thrusting his hand into the pocket of the fellow, he drew from it the three sovereigns and the three shillings he had paid him for his boat and his information. It was evident enough now that he belonged to the Reindeer, and that he had been sent out by Captain Stopfoot to do precisely what he had done, taking advantage of the general good feeling which prevailed between the negroes and the Union forces.

Christy thought that Captain Stopfoot had been over-confident to leave his prisoners without a guard; but it appeared now that Quimp had been employed in this capacity, though it was probable that he had been instructed not to show himself to them, and for that reason had crept to his station and lain down on the deck.

"Now, my men, take your arms from that bale of cotton; but don't make any noise," said Christy in a low tone, as he took his revolvers and cutlass from the heap of weapons; and the seamen promptly obeyed the order. "The captain of this steamer managed his affair very well indeed, and I intend to adopt his tactics."

The steamer was under way, and had been for some time. Christy climbed upon the bales of cotton far enough to see what the crew of the vessel were doing. The hatches appeared to have been taken off in the waist and forward, and the crew were lowering cargo into the hold. A portion of the cotton had either been hoisted out of the hold, or had been left on deck, to form the hiding-places for the men. The captain must have had early notice of the approach of the Bellevite and Bronx; but there had been time enough after the former began to fire at the battery to enable him to make all his preparations.

Captain Stopfoot was not to be seen, and was probably in the pilothouse. The officer concluded that there must be as many as four men in the hold attending to the stowage of the bales, and four more could be seen tumbling the cargo through the hatches. This accounted for eight men; and this was the number Christy had figured out as the crew of the Reindeer, though there was doubtless a man at the wheel. The force was about equal to his own, not counting the engineers and the firemen.

Christy stationed his men as he believed Captain Stopfoot had arranged his force. The cabin was in a deck-house; between the door of it and the piles of cotton was a vacant space of about six feet fore and aft, which could not be overlooked from the forward part of the vessel. It was here that the first movement had been made. Calwood, who had been on duty here, said that two men had dropped down upon them; and when the third man came to learn the cause of the disturbance, he had been secured by two more.

This was the noise that Christy had heard when he sent two hands from the forecastle to ascertain the occasion of it. The three prisoners had been disarmed, bound, and concealed in the cabin. They were threatened with instant death if they made any outcry, and one of their own revolvers was pointed at them. Linman, who had been sent to learn what had become of Hopkins and White, was treated in the same manner. Then he went himself, and the mate had dropped upon him, while those from under the bales secured Bench and Kingman.

Every sailor was fully instructed in regard to the part he was to have in the programme, and Christy had crawled forward to the point where he found the aperture in which Groomer, the mate, had been concealed. He was followed by Norlock, a very powerful man, who was to "make the drop" on Captain Stopfoot, and stuff a handkerchief into his mouth before he could call for assistance. Christy believed that the commander would be the first one to come aft when the men by the cabin fired their revolvers, as they had been instructed to do.

Two hands had been placed where they could fall upon the two who were rolling the cotton into the hold at the hatch in the waist; and two more were instructed to rush forward and fall upon the two men at work at the fore-hatch. The four men in the space in front of the cabin were to leap upon the bales and rush forward, revolvers in hand, and secure those at work in the hold. If there was any failure of the plan to work as arranged, the sailors were to rally at the side of their officer, ready for a stand-up fight.

Christy gave the signal for the two revolvers to be discharged. The captain did not appear at the report of the arms as expected; but he ordered the two hands at work at the after-hatch to go aft and look out for the prisoners. The two seamen on that side of the steamer dropped upon them, gagged them, and secured them so quickly that they could hardly have known what had happened to them. The enterprise had been inaugurated without much noise; but the captain had heard it, and called one of the men at the fore-hatch to take the wheel, from which it appeared that he had been steering the steamer himself.

The naval officer saw this man enter the pilot-house, from which Captain Stopfoot had come out. He moved aft quite briskly with a revolver in his hand; but as soon as he had reached the point where the mate had dropped upon him, Christy leaped upon his head and shoulders, and he sank to the deck, borne down by the weight of his assailant. He was surprised, as the first victim of the movement had been, and a handkerchief was stuffed into his mouth. He had dropped his weapon, which Christy picked up and discharged while his knees were placed on the chest of the prostrate commander, and his left hand grappled his throat. He was conquered as quickly as the first victim had been.

The shots had been the signal for all not engaged to rally at the side of the lieutenant, and the men rushed forward. All of them had removed their neck handkerchiefs to serve as gags, and they brought with them the lines with which they had been bound. The captain was rolled over, and his arms tied behind him. He was sent aft to the cabin, while Christy led six of his crew forward. The hands in the

Fighting for the Right

hold had attempted to come on deck, but the two sailors at each hatch dropped upon them.

In less than five minutes every one of the crew of the Reindeer had been "jumped upon, " as the sailors put it, bound, and marched to the cabin. The battle was fought and the victory won. Christy was quite as happy as Captain Stopfoot had been when he had taken possession of the steamer. The man at the wheel had been the last to be secured, and Calwood was put in his place, with directions to come about and steer for Egmont Key.

Christy determined not to make the mistake Captain Stopfoot had committed in leaving his prisoners insufficiently guarded. He selected four of his best men, ordered them to hold the cutlass in the right hand and the revolver in the left, and to keep their eyes on the prisoners all the time. He then went to those who had been gagged, and removed the handkerchiefs from their mouths.

"I am as grateful to you, Captain Stopfoot, as you were to me less than an hour ago, " said Christy, and he removed the gag from his mouth. "I am happy to be able to reciprocate your complimentary speeches. "

"I am not aware that I have done anything to merit your gratitude, Mr. Passford, " said the chief prisoner.

"You are not? Why, my dear Captain, you could not have arranged everything better than you did for the recapture of the Reindeer, " replied Christy.

"I did not think that ten men with their hands tied behind them could do anything to help themselves; but you Yankees are very ingenious, and it seems that you found a way to liberate yourselves. Besides, I had a hand here to watch you, with instructions to call me if there was any trouble, " added the captain, in an apologetic tone.

"When the trouble came he was not in condition to call you, " the lieutenant explained.

"No, sar! Dem beggars gagged me, and den robbed me of all my money! " howled Quimp, whose greatest grievance was the loss of his fifteen dollars.

"That was hardly justifiable, Mr. Passford, " added the captain shaking his head.

"It would not have been justifiable if the rogue had not first swindled me out of the money, " replied the naval officer.

"How was that? " asked the chief prisoner.

Christy explained the manner in which he had encountered Quimp, saying that he had paid him five dollars for the loss of his boat, and ten for the information that a steamer was loaded with cotton and ready to sail behind the long key.

"Quimp is as smart as a Yankee, " said Captain Stopfoot, laughing in spite of his misfortune. "The flatboat was one we picked up on one of the keys; and the information was precisely what I instructed Quimp to give you, without money and without price. I promised to give him ten dollars if he would pretend to be an honest nigger, and do the job properly. I have no fault to find with him; but under present circumstances I have not ten dollars to give him. I have lost the steamer and the cotton, and it seems to be all up with me. "

"I hope you will get into a safer business, Captain. I will suggest to the commander of the Bellevite that you and your party be landed at Gasparilla Pass; and I shall thus be able to reciprocate your good intentions towards me. "

Christy had sent some of his men forward, and he now followed them himself. The engineers had remained in their room, and kept the machinery in motion. As the Reindeer approached Egmont Key, the Bellevite, followed by the Bronx towing a schooner, were discovered coming out of the bay.

It was evident that the second lieutenant's capture had not been the only one during the day, and he concluded that Mr. Lobscott had brought out the schooner that had been supposed to be at Piney Point.

The Reindeer was about two miles south of Egmont Key when the Bellevite came out of the bay, and the latter stopped her screw as soon as she had reached a favorable position a mile from the island. Christy brought his prize as near to her as it was prudent to go in the open sea. The lieutenant went to the cabin to look out for the

Fighting for the Right

prisoners there, and found that the four men who had been detailed a guard were marching up and down the cabin in front of their charge, plainly determined that the steamer should not be captured again.

"Boat from the Bellevite, sir, " said one of the men on the quarter.

"Where is the Bronx and her prize now, Kingman? " asked Christy.

"Just coming by the island, sir. "

In a few minutes more the third cutter of the Bellevite came alongside. Mr. Walbrook, the third lieutenant of the ship, came on board of the Reindeer, and touched his cap to his superior officer.

"Captain Breaker requests you to report on board of the ship, and I am directed to take charge of the prize you have captured, Mr. Passford. "

"I will go on board at once, Mr. Walbrook, " replied Christy. "It is necessary for me to inform you before I leave that this steamer has changed hands twice to-day, and her ship's company have given me a great deal of trouble. The prisoners are in the cabin under guard, and I must caution you to be vigilant. Calwood will inform you in regard to the particulars. "

"I am sorry to inform you that Mr. Blowitt was severely, if not dangerously wounded in the action with the battery up the bay, where we had some sharp work, " added Mr. Walbrook.

"That is very bad news to me, " replied Christy, who had known the wounded man as second officer of the Bellevite when she was his father's yacht, and had served under him when she became a man-of-war, and as his first lieutenant in the Bronx.

The intelligence filled him with anxiety and sorrow; but while he was fighting for the right, as he had been for three years, he could not give way to his feelings. Without asking for the result of the action up the bay, he went over the side into the cutter, and ordered the crew to pull for the ship. Mr. Blowitt had been more than his superior officer, he had been his friend, and the young lieutenant was very sad while he thought of the wounded officer.

He found Captain Breaker on the quarter-deck; and he could see from his expression that he was greatly affected by the condition of his executive officer. Mr. Dashington, his first officer in the yacht, had been killed in action the year before, and now another of his intimate associates might soon be registered in the Valhalla of the nation's dead who had perished while fighting for the right.

"We have sad news for you, Mr. Passford, " said the commander, who seemed to be struggling with his emotions.

"But I hope there is a chance for Mr. Blowitt's recovery, Captain Breaker, " added Christy.

"I am afraid there is not. Dr. Linscott has very little hope that he will live. But we have no time to mourn even for our best friends. You have captured a steamer and brought her out; but I saw that you were coming up from the southward when I first discovered the steamer. What does that mean, Mr. Passford? "

"I hardly know, Captain, whether I brought her out, or she brought me out, " replied Christy, who felt very tender over the Southern Yankee trick which had been played upon him. "The steamer is the Reindeer, Captain Stopfoot. My boat's crew were overpowered by her ship's company, and we were all made prisoners; but we rebelled against the humiliating circumstances, and recaptured the steamer. "

"Then you have redeemed yourself, " added the captain.

Christy gave a detailed report of all the events that had occurred during his absence from the ship. The commander listened to him with the deepest interest; for the young officer was in some sense his *protégé*, and had sometimes been his instructor in navigation and seamanship. In spite of the sadness of the hour, there was a smile on his face when he comprehended the scheme of the captain of the Reindeer to get his vessel out of the bay in the face of two men-of-war.

While Christy was still on the quarter-deck, Mr. Lobscott came on board, and reported the capture of the schooner Sylphide, full of cotton. Her ship's company, consisting of six men, were on board of the Bronx. Captain Breaker planked the deck for some time, evidently making up his mind what to do with the prizes and with their crews, for he did not regard these men as prisoners of war. He asked the second lieutenant some questions in regard to the character of the Reindeer. She was an old-fashioned craft, but a good vessel.

"We are rather overburdened with prisoners, and I desire only to get rid of them, " said the captain.

"Captain Stopfoot was considerate enough to announce his intention to put me and my men on shore at Gasparilla Pass; and I promised to reciprocate the favor by suggesting that he and his ship's company be landed at the same place. "

"That will be a good way to get rid of them, and I will adopt the suggestion, " replied the commander.

All the rest of the day and a part of the night were used up in making the preparations for disposing of the prizes. A large number of hands were sent on board of the Reindeer, and her cotton was nearly all placed in the hold by good stowage. The prisoners from both prizes, except the engineers and firemen, who were willing to work for wages, were transferred to the Bronx. Mr. Lobscott was appointed prize-master of the steamer, which was to tow the schooner to Key West, where both were to be disposed of as circumstances might require.

The Bronx was to convoy the two vessels as far as the Pass, where she was to land her prisoners, and then return to her consort. At midnight this fleet sailed. A protest against being landed at the place indicated came from Captain Stopfoot before it departed; but the commander paid no attention to it, declaring that if the Pass was good enough for one of his officers, it was good enough for the captain of a blockade-runner.

"Mr. Passford, by the lamentable accident to Mr. Blowitt, you become the ranking lieutenant in condition for service, " said Captain Breaker, soon after the young officer had reported the capture of the Reindeer. "You therefore become the acting executive officer of the Bellevite. "

"Of course I shall do my duty faithfully, Captain Breaker, in whatever position is assigned to me, " replied Christy, his bosom swelling with emotion. "I regret more than anything else the occasion that makes it necessary to put me in this place; and I am very sorry to be called upon to occupy a position of so much responsibility."

"You are competent to discharge the duties of executive officer, Mr. Passford, though I appreciate your modesty in not desiring such an important position; but there is no alternative at present."

It was therefore under Christy's direction that all the arrangements for sending off the prizes were made. The Bronx returned at noon the next day, and both vessels sailed to the station of the flag-officer. The commander reported that he had silenced two batteries, captured a steamer and a schooner, sending them to Key West; but the shoal water in the vicinity of Tampa had prevented him from capturing the town.

Christy, in becoming first lieutenant, was relieved from duty as a watch officer; but his duties and responsibilities had been vastly increased. He was the second in command, and a shot from another vessel or a battery on shore might make him the commander, and he certainly did not aspire to such a charge and such an honor. There was something in the situation that worried him greatly. Captain Breaker had not been to the North since he entered upon his duties, now very nearly three years, and the state of his health had given Dr. Linscott considerable uneasiness.

Mr. Blowitt was sent home by a store-ship; but he died soon after his arrival; and his loving companions-in-arms could not follow his remains to an honored grave.

The flag-officer, either because he believed that Christy was a faithful and competent officer, in spite of his age, though in this respect he had added a year to his span, or that no other officer was available for the vacant position, made no other appointment, and Christy was compelled to retain the place, very much against his desire. As he thought of it he was absolutely astonished to find himself, even temporarily, in so exalted a position.

Here we are obliged to leave him for the present, crowned with honors far beyond his most sanguine expectations, but always willing to do his duty while fighting for the right. The future was still before him; he had not yet done all there was for him to do; and in the early years of his manhood came his reward, in common with the loyal sons of the nation, in A VICTORIOUS UNION.

OLIVER OPTIC'S BOOKS

+All-Over-the-World Library. + By OLIVER OPTIC. First Series. Illustrated.

1. +A Missing Million+; or, The Adventures of Louis Belgrade.
2. +A Millionaire at Sixteen+; or, The Cruise of the "Guardian Mother."
3. +A Young Knight Errant+; or, Cruising in the West Indies.
4. +Strange Sights Abroad+; or, Adventures in European Waters.

No author has come before the public during the present generation who has achieved a larger and more deserving popularity among young people than "Oliver Optic." His stories have been very numerous, but they have been uniformly excellent in moral tone and literary quality. As indicated in the general title, it is the author's intention to conduct the readers of this entertaining series "around the world." As a means to this end, the hero of the story purchases a steamer which he names the "Guardian Mother," and with a number of guests she proceeds on her voyage. —*Christian Work, N.Y.*

+All-Over-the-World Library. + By OLIVER OPTIC. Second Series. Illustrated..

1. +American Boys Afloat+; or, Cruising in the Orient.
2. +The Young Navigator+; or, The Foreign Cruise of the "Maud."
3. +Up and Down the Nile+; or, Young Adventurers in Africa.
4. +Asiatic Breeze+; or, Students on the Wing.

The interest in these stories is continuous, and there is a great variety of exciting incident woven into the solid information which the book imparts so generously and without the slightest suspicion of dryness. Manly boys will welcome this volume as cordially as they did its predecessors. —*Boston Gazette.*

+All-Over-the-World Library. + By OLIVER OPTIC. Third Series. Illustrated..

1. +Across India+; or, Live Boys in the Far East.
2. +Half Round the World+; or, Among the Uncivilized.
3. +Four Young Explorers+; or, Sight-Seeing in the Tropics.
4. +Pacific Shores+; or, Adventures in Eastern Seas.

Amid such new and varied surroundings it would be surprising indeed if the author, with his faculty of making even the commonplace attractive, did not tell an intensely interesting story of adventure, as well as give much information in regard to the distant countries through which our friends pass, and the strange peoples with whom they are brought in contact. This book, and indeed the whole series, is admirably adapted to reading aloud in the family circle, each volume containing matter which will interest all the members of the family. —*Boston Budget*.

OLIVER OPTIC'S BOOKS

+Army and Navy Stories. + By OLIVER OPTIC. Six volumes. Illustrated. Any volume sold separately..

1. +The Soldier Boy+; or, Tom Somers in the Army.
2. +The Sailor Boy+; or, Jack Somers in the Navy.
3. +The Young Lieutenant+; or, Adventures of an Army Officer.
4. +The Yankee Middy+; or, Adventures of a Navy Officer.
5. +Fighting Joe+; or, The Fortunes of a Staff Officer.
6. +Brave Old Salt+; or, Life on the Quarter Deck.

"This series of six volumes recounts the adventures of two brothers, Tom and Jack Somers, one in the army, the other in the navy, in the great Civil War. The romantic narratives of the fortunes and exploits of the brothers are thrilling in the extreme. Historical accuracy in the recital of the great events of that period is strictly followed, and the result is, not only a library of entertaining volumes, but also the best history of the Civil War for young people ever written. "

+Boat Builders Series. + By OLIVER OPTIC. In six volumes. Illustrated. Any volume sold separately..

1. +All Adrift+; or, The Goldwing Club.
2. +Snug Harbor+; or, The Champlain Mechanics.
3. +Square and Compasses+; or, Building the House.
4. +Stem to Stern+; or, Building the Boat.
5. +All Taut+; or, Rigging the Boat.
6. +Ready About+; or, Sailing the Boat.

"The series includes in six successive volumes the whole art of boat building, boat rigging, boat managing, and practical hints to make the ownership of a boat pay. A great deal of useful information is

Fighting for the Right

given in this +Boat Builders Series+, and in each book a very interesting story is interwoven with the information. Every reader will be interested at once in Dory, the hero of 'All Adrift, ' and one of the characters retained in the subsequent volumes of the series. His friends will not want to lose sight of him, and every boy who makes his acquaintance in 'All Adrift' will become his friend."

+Riverdale Story Books. + By OLIVER OPTIC. Twelve volumes. Illustrated..

1. +Little Merchant.+
2. +Young Voyagers.+
3. +Christmas Gift.+
4. +Dolly and I.+
5. +Uncle Ben.+
6. +Birthday Party.+
7. +Proud and Lazy.+
8. +Careless Kate.+
9. +Robinson Crusoe, Jr.+
10. +The Picnic Party.+
11. +The Gold Thimble.+
12. +The Do-Somethings.+

+Riverdale Story Books. + By OLIVER OPTIC. Six volumes. Illustrated.

1. +Little Merchant.+
2. +Proud and Lazy.+
3. +Young Voyagers.+
4. +Careless Kate.+
5. +Dolly and I.+
6. +Robinson Crusoe, Jr.+

+Flora Lee Library. + By OLIVER OPTIC. Six volumes. Illustrated.

1. +The Picnic Party.+
2. +The Gold Thimble.+
3. +The Do-Somethings.+
4. +Christmas Gift.+
5. +Uncle Ben.+
6. +Birthday Party.+

These are bright short stories for younger children who are unable to comprehend the +Starry Flag Series+ or the +Army and Navy Series+. But they all display the author's talent for pleasing and interesting the little folks. They are all fresh and original, preaching no sermons, but inculcating good lessons.

OLIVER OPTIC'S BOOKS

+The Great Western Series. + By OLIVER OPTIC. In six volumes. Illustrated..

1. +Going West+; or, The Perils of a Poor Boy.
2. +Out West+; or, Roughing it on the Great Lakes.

3. +Lake Breezes+; or, The cruise of the Sylvania.
4. +Going South+; or, Yachting on the Atlantic Coast.
5. +Down South+; or, Yacht Adventures in Florida.
6. +Up the River+; or, Yachting on the Mississippi.

"This is the latest series of books issued by this popular writer, and deals with life on the Great Lakes, for which a careful study was made by the author in a summer tour of the immense water sources of America. The story, which carries the same hero through the six books of the series, is always entertaining, novel scenes and varied incidents giving a constantly changing yet always attractive aspect to the narrative. OLIVER OPTIC has written nothing better."

+The Yacht Club Series. + By OLIVER OPTIC. In six volumes. Illustrated.

1. +Little Bobtail+; or, The Wreck of the Penobscot.
2. +The Yacht Club+; or, The Young Boat Builders.
3. +Money-Maker+; or, The Victory of the Basilisk.
4. +The Coming Wave+; or, The Treasure of High Rock.
5. +The Dorcas Club+; or, Our Girls Afloat.
6. +Ocean Born+; or, The Cruise of the Clubs.

"The series has this peculiarity, that all of its constituent volumes are independent of one another, and therefore each story is complete in itself. OLIVER OPTIC is, perhaps, the favorite author of the boys and girls of this country, and he seems destined to enjoy an endless popularity. He deserves his success, for he makes very interesting stories, and inculcates none but the best sentiments, and the 'Yacht Club' is no exception to this rule." —*New Haven Journal and Courier.*

+Onward and Upward Series+. By OLIVER OPTIC. In six volumes. Illustrated.

1. +Field and Forest+; or, The Fortunes of a Farmer.
2. +Plane and Plank+; or, The Mishaps of a Mechanic.
3. +Desk and Debit+; or, The Catastrophes of a Clerk.
4. +Cringle and Crosstree+; or, The Sea Swashes of a Sailor.
5. +Bivouac and Battle+; or, The Struggles of a Soldier.
6. +Sea and Shore+; or, The Tramps of a Traveller.

"Paul Farringford, the hero of these tales, is, like most of this author's heroes, a young man of high spirit, and of high aims and correct principles, appearing in the different volumes as a farmer, a captain, a bookkeeper, a soldier, a sailor, and a traveller. In all of them the hero meets with very exciting adventures, told in the graphic style for which the author is famous."

+The Lake Shore Series+. By OLIVER OPTIC. In six volumes. Illustrated..

1. +Through by Daylight+; or, The Young Engineer of the Lake Shore Railroad.
2. +Lightning Express+; or, The Rival Academies.
3. +On Time+; or, The Young Captain of the Ucayga Steamer.
4. +Switch Off+; or, The War of the Students.
5. +Brake Up+; or, The Young Peacemakers.
6. +Bear and Forbear+; or, The Young Skipper of Lake Ucayga.

"OLIVER OPTIC is one of the most fascinating writers for youth, and withal one of the best to be found in this or any past age. Troops of young people hang over his vivid pages; and not one of them ever learned to be mean, ignoble, cowardly, selfish, or to yield to any vice from anything they ever read from his pen." —*Providence Press*.

OLIVER OPTIC'S BOOKS

+The Famous Boat Club Series. + By OLIVER OPTIC. Six volumes. Illustrated.

1. +The Boat Club+; or, The Bunkers of Rippleton.
2. +All Aboard+; or, Life on the Lake.
3. +Now or Never+; or, The Adventures of Bobby Bright.
4. +Try Again+; or, The Trials and Triumphs of Harry West.
5. +Poor and Proud+; or, The Fortunes of Katy Redburn.
6. +Little by Little+; or, The Cruise of the Flyaway.

"This is the first series of books written for the young by OLIVER OPTIC. It laid the foundation for his fame as the first of authors in which the young delight, and gained for him the title of the Prince of Story Tellers. The six books are varied in incident and plot, but all are entertaining and original."

+Young America Abroad+: A Library of Travel and Adventure in Foreign Lands. By OLIVER OPTIC. Illustrated by Nast and others. First Series. Six volumes.

Fighting for the Right

1. +Outward Bound+; or, Young America Afloat.
2. +Shamrock and Thistle+; or, Young America in Ireland and Scotland.
3. +Red Cross+; or, Young America in England and Wales.
4. +Dikes and Ditches+; or, Young America in Holland and Belgium.
5. +Palace and Cottage+; or, Young America in France and Switzerland.
6. +Down the Rhine+; or, Young America in Germany.

"The story from its inception, and through the twelve volumes (see Second Series), is a bewitching one, while the information imparted concerning the countries of Europe and the isles of the sea is not only correct in every particular, but is told in a captivating style. OLIVER OPTIC will continue to be the boys' friend, and his pleasant books will continue to be read by thousands of American boys. What a fine holiday present either or both series of 'Young America Abroad' would be for a young friend! It would make a little library highly prized by the recipient, and would not be an expensive one." — *Providence Press*.

+Young America Abroad. + By OLIVER OPTIC. Second Series. Six volumes. Illustrated.

1. +Up the Baltic+; or, Young America in Norway, Sweden, and Denmark.
2. +Northern Lands+; or, Young America in Russia and Prussia.
3. +Cross and Crescent+; or, Young America in Turkey and Greece.
4. +Sunny Shores+; or, Young America in Italy and Austria.
5. +Vine and Olive+; or, Young America in Spain and Portugal.
6. +Isles of the Sea+; or, Young America Homeward Bound.

"OLIVER OPTIC is a *nom de plume* that is known and loved by almost every boy of intelligence in the land. We have seen a highly intellectual and world-weary man, a cynic whose heart was somewhat embittered by its large experience of human nature, take up one of OLIVER OPTIC's books, and read it at a sitting, neglecting his work in yielding to the fascination of the pages. When a mature and exceedingly well-informed mind, long despoiled of all its freshness, can thus find pleasure in a book for boys, no additional words of recommendation are needed." — *Sunday Times*.

* * * * * * * * * * * * *

Copyright © 2021 Esprios Digital Publishing. All Rights Reserved.

CPSIA information can be obtained
at www.ICGtesting.com
Printed in the USA
BVHW082258030122
625358BV00003B/27

9 781006 076114